MW00772514

The

Arts of
Seduction

The
Arts of
Seduction

Seema Anand

ALEPH

ALEPH

ALEPH BOOK COMPANY
An independent publishing firm
promoted by *Rupa Publications India*

First published in India in 2018
by Aleph Book Company
7/16 Ansari Road, Daryaganj
New Delhi 110 002

ISBN: 978-93-86021-91-5

15 17 19 20 18 16 14

Printed in India

To my bubbas,
Tarini, Varun and Nikhil

The right to feel pleasure
The right to tell your story
And the right to choose to do so...

Here's to changing the world, one little story at a time.

Contents

Introduction

'So long as lips shall kiss, and eyes shall see,
so long lives This, and This gives life to Thee...'
—Kama Sutra[*]

This book is a guide to having great sex in the twenty-first century. It seeks to transform what has largely been reduced to instant gratification into a rather more sensuous experience.

My motivation in writing this book is best summed up by this response by Dr Alex Comfort (translator of the *Ananga Ranga*) to a reader in the *New Statesman*: 'Mr. Simon Raven finds sex an "overrated sensation which lasts a bare ten seconds"—and then wonders why anyone should bother to translate the erotic textbooks of medieval India. One good reason for doing so is that there are still people in our culture who find sex an overrated sensation lasting a bare ten seconds....'

'Mr. Simon Raven' wasn't alone in his way of thinking. Someone recently said to me, 'All this seduction stuff is crap.

---

[*]The Kama Sutra of Vatsyayana, translated from the Sanskrit by Sir Richard Francis Burton, Kama Shastra Society of London and Benares, 1883.

Sex is hot and fast. When a lion has sex the female knows it...' Except, we are not animals. Yes, it is possible to throw yourself on top of your partner and hammer your way to an ejaculation in a matter of seconds but, as journalist and author Yasmin Alibhai Brown says, 'there is a difference between a fuck and [an] experience'.

In order to elevate our animal instincts to a more refined form of pleasure, I turned to the *Kama Sutra*, which remains a groundbreaking work thousands of years after it was written. The *Kama Sutra,* compiled by Vatsayayan some time in the third century, is the oldest and most notable of a group of texts on erotic love from ancient India known generically as the Kama Shastras. The *Kama Sutra* goes deep into the art of making love, and shows how it can be sophisticated and hugely enjoyable. It offers every permutation of every act of foreplay and lovemaking. After all, we as humans are the only species on earth capable of consciously creating and enjoying mutual pleasure. And it wasn't just momentary physical pleasure— ancient Eastern cultures believed that a stable society depended on a stable marriage and the secret to a stable marriage was extremely good sex. Marriage was the path to heaven and sex was the vehicle to get you there, and therefore the *Kama Sutra*—and its fellow manuals—were considered works of divine instruction.[*]

What makes the *Kama Sutra* stand out from other similar texts is that in compiling the book, Vatsyayan did what no one had ever done before—he broke the ultimate gender myth. For

---

[*]'The union of man and woman is like the mating of heaven and earth. It is because of their correct mating that heaven and earth last forever. Human beings have lost this secret and have therefore become mortal. By knowing it, the path to immortality is opened...'—Shang-Ku-San-Tai

centuries religious belief had held that a woman did not have an independent source of pleasure, that her pleasure depended on that of the man—in other words, a woman's orgasm was the result of a man's orgasm. The *Kama Sutra* stated that not only do women have an independent source of pleasure but that a man is not even necessary to the process. This belief was so controversial at the time that it created a huge stir; more importantly, it put the book on the map for all time.

However, as the centuries passed, the *Kama Sutra* got lost in the fog of prevailing attitudes and the mire of mistranslations. In the twentieth century, Freud reiterated the antediluvian idea that a woman can only achieve orgasm through regular sex with a man (an idea that the *Kama Sutra* had discarded almost 2,000 years ago)—any other kind of orgasm was of no real significance; in his words it was 'immature'. So a woman's sexuality—that spans an incredible spectrum of pleasure, fulfilment and potential—was reduced to an undifferentiated entity that revolved around the instant gratification of the male. Everything else was dysfunctional. The result was a whole century of sexual angst. And even though we now know better, attitudes are hard to shift.

⁌

Perhaps the real deciding factor, if I had to pick one, as to why I would like to introduce the *Kama Sutra* to people in the twenty-first century is its language. Far from the crudely misogynistic and downright abusive vocabulary that has come to be associated with sexual practices, the language of the *Kama Sutra* (as well as all the literature it inspired over the following 1,500 years) is characterized by a degree of refinement, beauty and nuanced pleasure, which even extends to the words used to describe women's genitalia—the clitoris is referred to as the 'madan-chhatri' or the 'love umbrella', the vulva is the 'chandan-mahal' or the 'fragrant palace'. If the words that we use define our actions, then this is certainly a book that is very deliberately leading us away from the gratuitous violence of imagined passions or the ennui of stale sex towards a world of pleasure where arousal happens one little nerve ending at a time. As feminist Naomi Wolf has said, 'Just imagine how differently a young girl today might feel about her developing womanhood if every routine slang description she heard of female genitalia used metaphors of preciousness and beauty, and every account of sex was centred on her pleasure—pleasure on which the general harmony depended.' [*]

Alongside India, ancient China also had a prominent culture of erotic treatises. A few thousand years ago, borders were not quite as sharp as they are now and there was a surprising exchange of information and ideologies between the two cultures. Both viewed sex and sensuality as essential to the human condition. Both promoted the experience of sexual ecstasy as the vehicle to heaven. Both disseminated it as a medical science, teaching the healing and therapeutic effects of sex.

Of the differences, however, the most important one according to me was that while the Chinese manuals concentrate on the sexual act (detailing the number of thrusts, levels of bodily fluids, the length of time for penetration, etc.) the Indian treatises focus on foreplay and seduction—how to develop the perfect mood before and after sex. Seduction was considered

---

[*]Naomi Wolf, *Promiscuities: The Secret Struggle for Womanhood*, New York: Random House, 1997, p. 183.

an art and, when practiced carefully, it benefited the mind, the body and the soul because it gradually stirred up all the senses and activated the latent energy within us. Refinement was paramount—it elevated the human mind and prepared us for better things.

So why did the Indian treatises value the arts of seduction so much more over the actual act of sex?

Let me posit a couple of theories.

Not only did the finer arts of seduction elevate us from the level of the beasts, as I've said, they were very effective in harmonizing the sexual energy of lovers so that the sexual act became a mutually enjoyable experience. The ancients understood that men and women were completely different as lovers and if left to discover their own arousal there was almost no point at which their sexual energies would coincide.

Men's desires are like fire, starting at the genitals and moving up to the brain. They are easy to ignite and equally quick to extinguish. They need very little encouragement to arrive at full arousal and are content with instant gratification. Women's desires are like water, starting at the head and flowing downwards; and like water they take far longer to come to the boil and equally long to cool down.

The arts of seduction as prescribed by the *Kama Sutra*— with all its hundreds of rules and rituals—were meant to bridge the gap between the two sexes. They were meant to slow the man down and encourage him to take his time over his arousal and at the same time give the woman enough time and motivation to raise her sexual energies and desires.

The goal of seduction was more than just a meeting of two bodies—it involved every single sense, beginning with the most erogenous zone of all—the mind. That, according to the *Kama Sutra*, is the start and end of the road to sexual fulfilment.

And to stress this point—although the *Kama Sutra* invokes the blessings of Kamadeva (the god of love and desire)—the patron deity of the work is Saraswati, the goddess of music, literature, learning; because, as everyone knows, a man who is culturally well informed, the one who can stimulate your mind is the most attractive man of all.

My other theory is that the Indian arts of erotic love and seduction were created by a woman. Very early on in Hindu mythology, Kamadeva is killed off, incinerated by the great god Shiva in a moment of rage. You may not have consciously considered this, but we are the only culture in which Cupid (or Eros) doesn't have a physical body—he is ananga.*

After Kamadeva's death the gods convince his wife, Rati, to assume his duties. When she hears of her husband's death, a heartbroken Rati tries to kill herself but is dissuaded by the gods—the world cannot exist without love and desire. She agrees to carry on his very important work for the time being.

In the Indian context, playing Cupid is not as simple as running around shooting love arrows, it is a far more onerous task and involves teaching the refinements of the arts of love to interested parties so that they can be practised properly.

As you will discover, there is nothing utilitarian about the *Kama Sutra*. It is not a book about sex, but rather a vade mecum on the arts of seduction; this is a book about finesse and sophistication, about passion and skill, about the nuances of pleasure and depths of satisfaction—where arousal is a combination of physical intimacy and mental fantasy and everything is driven by an exquisite refinement.

In *The Arts of Seduction* I have made a careful selection of the best techniques of love and sex chosen from the wealth

---

*Ananga, 'formless' or 'without a body', is an epithet for Kamadeva.

of variations and ideas for seduction that the *Kama Sutra* has to offer—whether it is the innovative codes for love messages, the effects of applying perfume to different parts of the body, describing the many different types of kissing, where and how to massage your lover's feet or what kind of jewellery to wear during lovemaking—there's something for everyone here.

My main aim in writing this book is to make the idea of seduction part of everyday life. As Vatsyayan says, seduction is not an 'event'—it is not about 'doing' it for your partner, nor is it the exclusive property of people in relationships—seduction is for yourself, it should be a state of mind. Something that puts a spring in your step, a lilt in your voice and the fun into sex.

The *Kama Sutra*, although a treasure trove of the arts of seduction, is not an easy book to read, with its obscure references, obsolete materials and impossibly archaic language. I have shaped the information I wanted to disseminate into short, self-contained chapters so that readers can dip in and out depending on what interests them at different times. I want the reader to treat this as a handy guidebook for new and exciting experiences. Each chapter ends with a section titled 'My Advice' wherein I suggest ways in which to use some of the ideas discussed—to excite the mind, to share a laugh or to spice up your sex life. Whether you decide to begin a flirtation using paan or stimulate your own senses with perfume, my hope is that this book will irrevocably enrich your sex life.

The Art of Perfuming

Seduction begins with the art of perfuming the body.

Perfume was not meant to be merely dabbed and applied—it had to *be absorbed* into the skin and mingle with your perspiration to enhance your body's fragrance. Over the course of the day, as you perspired, the sweat would distil through the layer of scent and morph into an entirely new smell that was unique to you. This was you, your own personal scent, and it was this smell that had to be embedded in the consciousness of your lover and become reminiscent of all the things you had done together, so that each time you made love, your scent would stir up your lover's every sense with memories of past pleasures and anticipation of the delights to come. It is said that when Cleopatra set out to meet Mark Antony she had the sails of her barge soaked in perfume, so that even 'the winds were lovesick....'

∿

Perfuming was considered a very skilled craft in ancient India. Every part of the body had to be perfumed with a different fragrance—each scent was distinct and yet merged together like a shifting but composite whole; you could tell the fragrances apart but it was nearly impossible to know where one ended and the other began. It was an ocean of intoxicated senses with no room left for lucid thought. Seduction was not an event, it was a mood, a feeling, a desire that came from the soul and took time to build up. Perfume seduced the mind and the slow, languorous movements of warm scented oils being massaged into the body would bring a woman to a more advanced state of arousal and prepare her for a night of lovemaking.

Both men and women wore perfume but the perfuming rituals of women took longer and were far more complicated. For women, the perfuming was done after the bath and could take up several hours.

According to the *Kama Sutra,* the well of sexual desire sits in the parting on top of the head, so perfuming had to start with the hair. Traditionally, flirtation began with scented hair. If you wanted to attract a man's attention you would walk past him swishing your hair and leaving behind a trail of perfume. Or you could set up a rendezvous in the woods and then hide behind the trees, allowing the would-be lover to seek you out by following the scent of your hair.

Amongst the different perfumes used on hair, my favourite is khus or 'mitti attar'. Khus is literally the fragrance of the first rains falling on scorching hot soil. It is the ultimate aphrodisiac. Khus was applied to slightly wet hair very early in the morning before it was rolled up into a bun. Over the course of the day the perfume would seep into the hair, fuse with the perspiration and completely saturate the scalp so that by evening, when you opened your hair, you were a walking cloud of erotic promise—smelling of sun-baked earth and fresh rain.

Seema Anand

The neck was perfumed with a fresh scent, usually jasmine or tuberoses. These light scents were meant to conjure up an image of innocence and be the starting point for heavier scents that were concealed in the clandestine crevices and dimples further along the body. Jasmine was literally a sweet, 'non-intimidating' smell that encouraged the lover to come closer. In eighteenth-century France, jasmine became the perfume of the prostitutes because it made them smell clean and fresh and innocent—like the girl-next-door. This resulted in upper-class women not wanting to use it any more and so the heavier, more lush fragrances were created for them.

The breasts (or chest) were rubbed with a perfumed oil made of saffron and spiced cloves. Not only was the fragrance stronger but the saffron also served to even out the colour of the skin and make it glow.

The belly button was scented with musk—it was a small area and so it needed something heavier to draw the lover down to it.

The curve of the waist on the other hand was a larger space and so it was perfumed with the very subtle akund (crown flower). The curve of the waist was a road all lovers would have to travel; the perfume ensured that the journey didn't end too soon. In Indian mythology, the akund is one of the five flower arrows of Kamadeva and anyone who inhales this fragrance from the waist of the lover will be blessed with superior orgasms.

The arms and underarms were very important perfume spots. The arms were the largest exposed part of the body so they were perfumed as well as beautified. Makara (a magical animal like a dragon) designs were painted on the arms with perfumed civet powder.

The perfuming of the underarms was even more

complicated. According to the *Kama Sutra*, the armpit is a very important erogenous zone. There is a large erotic nerve that directly connects the underarm with the vulva and kissing the armpit stimulates the woman's love juices. There were several different embraces specifically created for the armpit and an entire array of perfumed oils, powders and substances have been suggested for this area.

The back was dotted with little dabs of sandalwood. Not rubbed over, just dotted in a series of loops because this created a trail for someone to follow. Like a game of treasure hunt, you could control where your lover began and finished the trail—often allowing it to end at a little hidden dimple or mole—the perfect prize for the lover's patience!

Perfumed breath was very important because the idea of kissing someone with bad breath was repulsive. Betel leaves, mango shoots, camphor, cloves etc. were used as mouth fresheners. Scented twigs were used for brushing the teeth every morning but before lovemaking men were advised to chew on lemon bark to freshen their mouth once again. But aside from this the lovers of the *Kama Sutra* were also advised to smoke specially scented cigarettes to perfume the mouth. Turning the myth of the after-sex cigarette on its head, the *Kama Sutra* suggests it should be smoked before lovemaking. The cigarette was to be rolled with fresh sandalwood, khus and oysters—a combination, we are told, that was a favourite of Kamadeva himself. Why a cigarette? The fragrant smoke would scent not just the mouth but the throat as well because the kisses and embraces recommended by the *Kama Sutra* were meant to go far deeper!

Perfume was a way of life. Clothes, bedrooms, bath water—everything was perfumed. The *Kama Sutra* even advises lovers to keep the distilled scents of cardamom and citrus by the bed at night in case the beloved fouled up the air by passing wind! There was no place for bad odours in the world of seduction.

Men were massaged vigorously with different perfumed oils just before their bath, an exercise that could take up to two hours—it was not just about scenting the body but also creating the right mood that would be arousing for his partner. After the bath, a little bit of extra scent was reapplied to specific parts of the body that were prone to more sweat—the emphasis being on 'little bit' because men of class only used small quantities of perfume. The amount of perfume you used was the difference in social status. Men of lower breeding used large quantities of scent, which caused them to reek of it.

Men also wore flower garlands of different types, all with their own fragrances, to check the smell of sweat on their brow and neck. The flowers were chosen according to the season, the time of day and the occasion. If he was going to a crowded mela where there was a chance of meeting the lover, the garland of choice would be of champa flowers—a strong, far-reaching fragrance—because this would attract the attention of the beloved as he walked past. For less crowded gatherings, he would wear a garland of jasmine which had a lighter scent. But 'for moments of amorous dalliance garlands of yellow amaranth flowers are recommended (even though they do not have any specific scent) since they do not fall during caressing, kissing or hugging.'*

At the time of the *Kama Sutra* the perfumes in fashion

---

*Alain Danielou (trans), *The Complete Kama Sutra*, New York: Simon and Schuster, 1993.

were musk, saffron, sandalwood, camphor, aloe, lemon, lavender, champa, juhi, kulaka, anjana and gorochana, the most popular of these being musk, amber, sandalwood and saffron because they smelled like the most intimate parts of a woman's body. (Obviously not such a bizarre idea since modern perfumers will tell you some of the most expensive perfumes on the shelves today are designed to smell like the vulva!)

Both men and women wore perfume and so both were expected to have a complete knowledge of this art—how to mix different fragrances, where on the body to use them, what was their effect on the senses etc.—because the right perfume applied to the precise spot could make your lover's brain do flip-flops that all the acrobatics in the world could not achieve.

The making and selling of perfume was a flourishing trade and aromatic resins were stored in the royal treasury like priceless gems. The art of perfuming was so important that Kautilya (the fourth-century forerunner to Machiavelli) devotes an entire chapter to it in his famous treatise, the *Arthashastra*.

My Advice

Perfume is like instant sexiness in a bottle. It has all the excitement of the unpredictable. When you mix two colours you know what you will get, when you mix two smells you have no idea what could happen. Use it to flirt, to seduce, to please your lover, to treat your own senses, to feel good!

If you are not a 'perfume person', now is the time to change that.

Perfume has an amazingly uplifting effect on your happy hormones. Good smells make you feel good!

Try the natural stuff. There are many expensive and fabulous perfume houses but good quality attar is on another stratosphere.

Natural oils are unspeakably romantic and silken and, to my mind, nothing manmade even comes close. Think about it—on the one hand you have the extract of crushed rose petals and on the other, there is civet (which is extracted from the butt of a rodent and is the base for the most expensive perfumes in the market today). Which story would you rather whisper?

Try musk attar. It has a heavy, sensuous tone.

Get khus. Khus, as I mentioned, is the smell of fresh rain as it falls on scorching hot soil. It originates in the little town of Kanauj in north India and is still made in exactly the same way as it was 3,000 years ago. Shallow ditches are dug and the earth in them is allowed to dry and harden and bake under the burning sun. Then the monsoons come and the rain water gradually soaks into the mud and takes on a whole new identity. The perfumers of Kanauj, with a magic that only they understand, distil this fragrance of rain-soaked mud and bottle it.

Don't just use it on the head, apply it to the skin, soak your pillow. with it It will transport you to a land of fantasy like nothing else can.

If natural oils are not practical for you, find yourself as good a quality perfume as you can afford. Don't buy cheap perfumes—they don't do the job.

Don't wear a perfume just because 'your friend uses it'—perfumes smell different on different people. Experiment with what suits you.

Perfume should never be used in overly large quantities but it has to be enough to have an impact.

If you are using perfume (as opposed to natural oils), I would not recommend mixing the fragrances on your skin—it doesn't have the same effect. But you can play around with them in different ways.

Perfume your handbag—get a perfume just for your

handbag and spray the inside so that every time you open it you get an expected whiff. It can really lift your mood.

Perfume your feet—this one is for both men and women. Spray the inside of your shoes with your favourite fragrance. You will be surprised at the result. The feet have the most number of nerve endings and they react very positively to perfume.

For the next special occasion try a game of perfume treasure hunt with your lover. Create perfume trails on your body and see where it leads.

Lovers' Quarrels

Nothing kills a relationship like the tedium of unremitting sweetness. All lovers need the adrenaline boost of a good old fight now and then to keep their love alive and healthy.

The author of the *Kama Sutra* seems to have felt so very strongly about the benefits of lovers' quarrels—in strengthening relationships and increasing passion—that he ends his section on foreplay and seduction with a chapter on lovers' quarrels.

All lovers must quarrel and fight regularly in order to keep the relationship fresh and exciting. Quarrels are not just things that happen, they *must* happen! It is as much a technique of romance as kissing and embracing.

The lovers' quarrel of the *Kama Sutra* was an out and out gloves-off fight and the making up—which was even more important—had to be done with pure, egoless, no-holds-barred love. But, Vatsyayan warns, lovers' quarrels only work for couples who share a very strong bond of love and trust, for those who understand that a quarrel is just a temporary bit of madness and that it has to be made up with even more love than the anger with which the fight started in the first place.

If a couple didn't share such a bond then the quarrel could

lead to further damage in the relationship.

Because the quarrels had a very specific purpose—to keep the relationship fresh and exciting and to increase the love between the couple—they had to be done in a very specific way and by following several rules, which Vatsyayan explains.

So what does the book of love say about lovers' quarrels?

According to the rules, the man starts the fight—by mentioning the name of another woman either during or just after sex. (According to the traditions of ancient Sanskrit poetry, quarrels arose from the actions of the man—he showed interest in some other woman or he was away too long or he seemed disinterested. This gave the woman the right to be angry and it became the man's role to appease her.)

Upon hearing the name of another woman, the beloved, who has been lying in his arms, enveloped in the warm glow of loving intimacy, is rudely jerked out of her mellowness. Vatsyayan says she is not to take this lying down—she is not a doormat or a martyr, she is a cherished lover—and she must react with all the security and entitlement of a cherished lover. She is to have a loud and unabashed tantrum.

The *Kama Sutra* says she must lash out at her lover in any and every way that she wishes, kicking him, screaming at him, breaking things, tearing off her jewellery and flinging it etc. She is the injured party and he needs to know it.

She can do pretty much anything she wants—except—and here's a very important rule—she cannot run out of the house. She can threaten to leave, she can run as far as the door, she can even stand at the doorframe and sulk—but she cannot run out of the house.

Why?

The *Kama Sutra* explains.

First, if she were to run out of the house and he did not

follow her immediately she would feel humiliated and it would not be easy for her to return with her dignity intact.

Secondly—and more importantly—as part of the making up, the man is supposed to fall at her feet, and it was forbidden for a man to fall at a woman's feet outdoors. This law was outlined by the sage Dattaka who, according to legend, created the rules of etiquette for social and sexual manners to be followed by lovers and courtesans.

Dattaka explains that the most popular position for lovemaking was the 'shulachitaka'—the woman lying flat on her back with one foot on her lover's head and the other on his shoulder. This would cause the alta* from beneath her feet to rub off on the man's forehead, and it seems that no matter how hard you scrubbed, the red marks had a tendency to not completely wash off. Somehow a little streak would always remain in the hair like a tell-tale sign (much like the twentieth-century 'lipstick on the collar'). If you saw a man with red marks on his forehead, you knew he was just returning from a visit to his lover.

The 'red marks on the forehead' became a metaphor for a man who had just had sex. It didn't have to be said—you knew! Ancient and medieval poets have used the red mark to describe the hurt silence (or tantrum) of many a heartbroken wife and the confusion of the husband who has been expecting a warm welcome and cannot understand her reaction.

So, a man placing her feet at his head was considered a very intimate act. A man only placed a woman's feet on his head when they made love. Since a lover's quarrel had to be made up

---

*Alta was a red paste with which all women traditionally adorned the soles of their feet—it was de rigueur. No woman would have ever considered setting out to have sex with unadorned feet.

with the man falling at the woman's feet—or in other words, with 'make up sex'—the quarrel could not be taken outdoors.

Having started the quarrel, the man must now make it up to her, with all the love and patience in the world, no matter how much time or effort it takes. He cannot get impatient or complain, he cannot say things like 'I've already apologized' or 'How many times are you going to repeat this' or 'Oh, for god's sake' etc. He needs to be abjectly repentant and cajole her back to good humour in an utterly loving and unquestioning manner.

The *Kama Sutra* says the man must throw himself at his lover's feet (this act of appeasement is known as 'pada patana') Because if he can do this—if he can be completely loving and repentant—at the end of this the beloved will feel so loved and cherished that she will want to return his love tenfold.

My Advice

Personally, I feel the chapter on lovers' quarrels is one of the soundest pieces of advice in the *Kama Sutra*. It is very relevant for our times.

Let us forget for a moment the grand tantrums, kicking and screaming. Just remember—fights happen and making up is essential. Vatsyayan has hit the nail on the head when he says that if the man can be intelligent enough to understand how to make up—without ego or pride, just putting his lady first—he will be blessed with the undying love and support of his partner and consequently have a life of blissful peace and harmony.

Fights are healthy now and again, but only so long as you understand that this is simply a difference of opinion, and they have to be made up in the end. It is so easy to fall into a rut and get buried under everyday matters and responsibilities: you talk less and less, problems simmer under the surface and become resentments. Nothing kills a relationship like the dreariness of deep-set monotony.

The occasional fight is a great way to clear the air and break that monotony.

However, the *Kama Sutra* is spot on when it says that this method of 'romancing' is for couples who share a deep love and trust. Because at the peak of the fight, when you are really furious, it is this love and trust that will bring you back to each other.

The making up has to be done with such complete openness, unfettered by the ego, that it leads you to fall in love with each other all over again.

Loud, all-out arguments are better than silent, sulky fights— they finish far quicker.

Don't storm out—stay and get it out of your system. And then look at your partner and remind yourself that you care for each other and have done so for a very long time and that this is just temporary insanity.

In telling us how to fight, in actually allocating roles, Vatsyayan once again proves that he is truly a master of the human psyche.

Other than the indisputable fact that we are of the same species, men and women are completely different physically, mentally and emotionally. We fight about different aspects of the same things and therefore the emotions and the focus of the fight is entirely different. This was obvious to a man living in the third century CE but still manages to elude the twenty-first century man by a mile.

Guys—if she is upset, don't tell her she's being silly or nagging or unreasonable. Accept that you've upset her—even if you are unable to understand why your actions could have had this effect—you need to be mature enough to know that you are partly responsible. Dump your ego and decide that it is you who will do the making up—and do it with complete and unconditional love. The returns will be beyond your expectations—focus on that.

Ladies—everyone expresses their emotions differently. If what he is doing to make up is not what you would have done in his place, do not hold that against him. Learn to read the signs of his love—the signs are there—appreciate them and love him back for it.

Do not burn any bridges. Lovers should quarrel, they should have the freedom to fight it out in whichever way they wish, but they should also have the maturity to understand the importance of boundaries.

Secret Language of Lovers

The *Kama Sutra* says that there are no words to express the delights of love, lovers and lovemaking. How do you convey what those few stolen moments meant to you, describe the passion of the night you spent together or put in words the exquisite anticipation of the meeting to come? Lovers' messages have to stretch across the domain of every fantasy and still create room for more.

For instance, a common trope in ancient Indian literature and the arts was the 'girdle of jingling bells'. It was not the norm for a woman to be on top during sex. For her to be on top, she had to be an exceptionally good lover—that is, she had to be good enough to bring herself and her partner to orgasm by only moving her hips. Not the torso, just the hips! And so, the really accomplished courtesans would wear a girdle of ghungroos around their upper waist and make sure that during sex none of the bells made a sound!

This jingling girdle became a symbol of erotic fantasy, a mood that was difficult to put into words—the sensation of the woman moving on top of her lover, the sight of her swinging breasts, the beads of sweat on her forehead and her earrings, grazing across her cheeks as she leaned forward to kiss her lover's lips; how would one describe the curtain of her hair as it fell across the lover's face—it was the 'jingling girdle' that said it all. If the man sent a jingling girdle as a gift to his mistress, she knew exactly what promises the evening held. If the poet said that she had put on her girdle, it was implicit that the woman had taken her position on top.

An expert knowledge of the secret love codes and symbols was one of the sixty-four essential skills of the *Kama Sutra* and indispensable to one's success in society and in love. Vatsyayan begins his chapter on the love codes with a grim warning to men who underestimate the importance of understanding these codes (as opposed to women, who clearly get their significance). He says a man can be rich, good looking and skilled in all the other sixty-three arts of love, but if he has no knowledge of the secret love codes then the woman of his dreams will dump him in the same way that one discards a wilted garland of flowers—in the garbage, without a second thought. If it became known that a man had been dumped by his lover, he would be destroyed socially. The *Kama Sutra* was not kidding when it said that one had to put aside everything else and 'study' the code with intensity and concentration because this code was like no other in history.

For one, this was a time before paper and pencil, so this whole code was not even entirely made up of words—it was a series of objects, gestures and symbols. For another, it was not just a private exchange between two individuals; this code had to serve every lover across the land in every conceivable situation. It needed a massive vocabulary that could cover every emotion and situation and it had to be nuanced enough to craft the message with all the delicacy and detail of a love letter, but without the use of words.

For instance, Bihari (a seventeenth-century poet) tells us, 'It was a religious festival. As the priests sit around the prayer fire he (our hero) picks up a lotus flower and looking at her (our heroine) touches the flower to his head. In response she lifts up her aarsi (ring with a mirror in the centre) and catching his reflection as well as the reflection of the sun in it, she puts it to her breast. He smiles and is content.'

The flower to the head means 'charan kamal' or 'your lotus feet'. A man would only have the woman's feet on his head after they made love (i.e. they are lovers). When our hero touches the lotus to his head after looking at his beloved, he is begging his lover to meet him that night. When she catches his reflection in her mirror ring, she is agreeing to meet with him. Catching the sun and then 'placing' it to her breast signifies that she will meet him after the sun has gone to rest in his mountain home.

Now if he had been ignorant of the love symbols....

ᶴ

The needs of lovers are endless and so are the symbols to express those needs. There was an entire range of love messages based on food and spices—cheap and easy to find.

To indicate love—a pouch of betel nut (hard supari) and catechu (katha).

Passionate love—cardamom, nutmeg and cloves.

In the grip of feverish passion—bamboo.

A booty call (I want you right now)—a bunch of grapes.

I am all yours—santol (cotton fruit).

I give you my life, sigh—cumin.

Be careful, I think someone suspects—wood apple (bilva).

It's okay, the danger has passed—haldi (turmeric).

In contrast, the most expensive and the most public love

messages were based on clothes—torn clothes—and this was specifically to express turbulent, frantic and uncontrollable emotions. Lacerated by the arrows of Kamadeva, you were so beside yourself that you went out in polite company in torn clothes. The more important and well known the beloved, the more expensive were the clothes you chose to wear—old and bad quality clothes would have been an insult to your love.

The clothes were strategically torn at the sleeves, the shoulders and the hem. One or two tears meant you were burning in the fire of extreme love, several tears (especially at the hem) depicted a breakup and re-sown patches with large visible stitches said you had made up and could not contain your joy.

The symbols and codes of love and lovers so captured the imagination of the poets and artists—this way of suggesting the actions of lovers rather than stating them—that very soon, the love codes of the *Kama Sutra* became the love language of the epic romances and miniature paintings of ancient and medieval India.

↗

Imagine this is the fourth century, a time before text messages and WhatsApp. The only place you are likely to run into your lover is at a crowded mela or festival and you have to use subtle gestures to have a very intimate conversation, to set up a date.

Using body language, this is how the conversation would go:

You are surrounded by hundreds of relatives and friends. Your eyes meet across the room.

You touch your ear—which means 'How are you?'

In response your lover touches the earlobe—'All the better for seeing you'.

Two hands to the heart and then one hand briefly to the head—'I'm going crazy thinking about you. When can we meet?'

At this point you hope that your beloved will run her fingers through her hair—running your fingers through your hair expressed erotic desire. If you were really lucky she would also curl a bit of hair around her index finger and pull it—that meant she was aroused and imagining a previous sexual encounter.

Thrilled with her reaction you now have to set up a date. This was the complicated bit and was done by counting the divisions on each finger (there are fourteen in total—three on each finger and two on the thumb). These represented the fourteen days of the fortnight, starting at the bottom-most division of the little finger for the first day of the moon and ending at the top of the thumb for the full moon. The nights of the waxing moon are indicated by the left hand and the waning moon by the right hand.

First, you would place your middle finger on top of your little finger and hold up your hand—that meant 'give me a date'. Then you would hold your hand up and start the count. When you got to the appropriate date, the beloved joined her hands together and held them up above her head and the date was set! Phew! Talk about logistics!

The next question would be 'where'. Generally, the meeting would take place at a rendezvous that the lovers had used previously. A raised thumb indicated the one to the east, the little finger the south, the middle finger west and the index north.

This secret exchange in a public place—of expressing attraction and arousal and setting up a rendezvous to slake that arousal—was as erotically charged as the physical act itself. The thought of sexual intimacy in public places, with the imminent fear of being caught at any time is obviously not a modern-day invention, it seems to have been a fantasy since the beginning of time.

~

Everything had its own meaning in the love code.

Women wore different pieces of jewellery to promise different positions and games of foreplay (see the chapter Jewellery and the Arts of Seduction). Similarly, men wore fresh flower garlands according to the season and the time of day to indicate their intentions. A garland of champa flowers was worn to get the attention of the beloved at a crowded festival—at the sight of the champa garland she would know he wanted her to sneak out somehow in order to meet him secretly. A garland of delicate jasmine flowers was to start a flirtation. A garland of amaranth flowers, as mentioned earlier, was for an 'amorous dalliance' because the flowers were very sturdy and would not shed 'during caressing, kissing or hugging'.

Some messages were one-word signals that were meant to be whispered into the beloved's ear as you passed her in the street, with no one else being any the wiser that a meeting had been set up. If your lover said 'ankush' (a hook-shaped goad used for training elephants), it meant he wanted to 'hook' up for the night. You could choose to accept—the word 'red' meant you accepted the meeting with love, 'yellow' said you accepted with passion, 'orange' said you accepted with indifference—'I will come and have sex with you, but frankly I could take it or leave it'. Or you could choose to say no—a firm 'wall' which was the modern day equivalent of 'talk to the hand'. And the dreaded 'black' which meant 'I despise you, don't even try calling me again.'

Love bites (see chapter Love Bites) and love scratches (see chapter Scratching in the Art of Lovemaking) had their own complex code of messages between lovers that were meant to arouse, to communicate, to remind and sometimes even to forget.

Possibly the most subtle and evocative was the love code of paan or betel leaf (see chapter Paan and the Arts of Seduction). Paan was offered as the very last thing in foreplay—to finish foreplay and begin sex. This particular paan was traditionally offered by the woman to her lover. If she filled it with a combination of valerian, jackfruit, camphor, cardamom and cloves stuck together with ginger paste, it meant that she was at the perfect state of arousal and he knew that the gates of ecstasy would open for him. There was a huge vocabulary in the giving and taking of paan—shapes, fillings, what time of night or day they were delivered, all carried their own message—messages unparalleled in romance, messages that could make your heart race and pulse stop.

The list of symbols was as unending and complex as the range of emotions that lovers can feel and there was a way to express them all.

My Advice

During his pre-election campaign, Warren Harding, the 29th President of the United States of America, sent his mistress, Carrie Fulton, a long list of code words which he explained they would now have to use in their letters to each other. The list included words like 'cloudy' which meant 'message not clear', 'repair' which meant 'I will meet you in New York' and (my favourite) 'grateful' which stood for 'all my love to the last precious drop'. As you can see, their code language was not just utilitarian—it had been carefully constructed to contain all the romance of a beautifully crafted love letter, and yet remain hidden from prying eyes.

For as long as time, lovers have been using secret languages to communicate with each other and express their desires. It is a tried and tested way to romance your partner.

Studies show that the more made-up and secret words for 'nooky' that lovers have between them the more playful and intimate their relationship tends to be.

It is arguably the easiest thing you can do to keep your romance going strong. A few secret words and inside jokes to share with your lover are incredible tools of closeness. It not only creates intimacy, but also an unseen periphery, a boundary wall within which to keep a relationship safe.

Do you have a secret word for your favourite position? Or for a personal moment?

Do you have a coded way to tell your lover, in public, that something has made you think of your most intimate moments together?

Do you have a collection of trigger words that can come up randomly in conversation and will take you both on a mutual flight of fantasy—your own little private fantasy—no matter how many people are around you?

Do you have certain objects or symbols that lead you to have mental sex?

No one spends all their time having (physical) sex—but having a mental and emotional connection is extremely exciting.

Lovers are advised to spend time creating their own secret code. Unfortunately, the extraordinary symbols and codes revealed in the text can no longer be used to set up a secret rendezvous because they have become public knowledge and are no longer 'secret'. The *Kama Sutra* advises that lovers spend time creating their own secret language because it is indispensable for a satisfying and successful relationship.

Love Bites

Just as the ocean is aroused into crashing waves by the rays of the moon so is the mind of the lover aroused by the sight of the beloved's throat framed by a necklace of love bites....

Just as the velvet flesh of the night is ornamented with stars which are the love bites of the moon, so is the body of the beloved covered with the jewels left by the lover's teeth.

The Kama Shastras are the only texts in the world that describe love bites in terms of romance and refinement, giving them the delicate and evocative vocabulary of a love letter. Lovers who express their mutual passion through love bites, the *Kama Sutra* says, will not see their love decay, even in a hundred years.

The love bite is generally described in unromantic headings. It is either the 'hickey', or worse, 'Odaxelagnia', which is its medical term. And let me sink the standards of romance just a little bit further by telling you that research into Odaxelagnia was obtained by studying donkeys biting each other's necks during sex!

But the *Kama Sutra* says love bites have an erotic currency that few other things can compare with. Of the six things that are done one after the other in order to build up passion (biting, scratching, moaning, sighing, etc.), love bites are at the top of the list. There is no sensation quite as exquisite as the feel of your lover's teeth on your already tingling and aroused flesh.

It is said that of all the arts of foreplay and seduction, the most amount of time and expertise went into creating the vocabulary for love bites. Even deciding what parts of the body were suitable for which bite took more debate than anything else in the ancient sexual treatises.

The *Kama Sutra* considers love bites to be one of the sixty-four essential skills that need to be learnt—with an emphasis on the word 'learnt'. Bites were part of the secret language of lovers—except not so secret—because love bites were meant to be seen. This was the world of court romances, everything was public and you were judged by your dexterity in the arts of love—biting being one such art.

Lovers left bite marks on each other as messages. The messages could be fairly simple, like 'I love you', or more complex, like 'I love you this much'.

There were different bite marks for different occasions—if one type of bite had the poignant passion of 'I am going away for a few months so the memory of this night will have to last me for a while', another had the excitement of reunion: 'I have just come back from a long journey and have been thinking of your body next to mine.'

They could indicate different seasons—a night of love under the monsoon full moon was different from stolen passion on a moonless spring night.

And most importantly, they had to be worthy of showing off. If the bite marks were clumsy or incorrect, that would bring dishonour to you and your lover (tantamount to social death!)—biting had to be done with precision and skill.

The first rule of biting was—you had to have good teeth. Only if you had good teeth were you allowed to leave love bites on your lover.

The *Kama Sutra* describes good teeth as even, with clean sharp edges, without gaps or chips, neither too big nor too small, shiny and white and with a surface that would easily absorb colour (from things like paan, betel leaf and black aloe paste). The fashion during the time of the *Kama Sutra* seems to have been for teeth that were coloured black or red—it's a fad that passed quickly, because by the fifth century there is no further mention of it. However, the idea of colouring the gums black, so that the teeth appear whiter, remained common practice even as late as the 1700s.

Bad teeth are described as blunt, decayed, overlapping or with wide spaces between them, uneven, chipped, too large or too small. Bite marks left with teeth like these were forbidden because they would bring dishonour to you and your lover.

The next consideration, and subject of lengthy discussions amongst ancient love experts, was where to bite your lover. After much debate, it was decided that love bites could be made on almost all the spots that were good for kissing except the eyes, the eyelids and the tongue. Further taboos depended on local customs—some people (but not all) forbade biting the forehead, the armpits, inside the vulva, and the penis.

How hard should the bite be? Here Vatsyayan takes a very firm stand. He says that biting could potentially cause injury and so it had to be monitored very carefully—any kind of force during sexual passion needs to be used under very strict controls, otherwise it can end in tragedy. The *Kama Sutra* tells us story after story about lovers who have maimed or even killed their partners in moments of blind, uncontrolled passion. When you are sexually aroused all logic is suspended and pain can seem very pleasurable, and so, it is important to keep it within strict boundaries. Each bite came with its own set of rules: how deep, how much of a mark, and so on.

Bites are made when the lovemaking has progressed. You never begin foreplay with love bites. They are for much later—when the heat is up, when passions are aroused, when orgasm is approaching. Anyone who starts biting their lover right at the beginning of foreplay, according to the *Kama Sutra*, is no better than a donkey in a rut.

There are ten main types of love bites.

Lovers are supposed to use the bite in the order of the pressure required.

The *Gudka* or *Discreet Bite* is the gentlest of the bites and it is made on the lower lip. Press your lover's lower lip gently but repeatedly with your teeth so that it becomes swollen and slightly red. The mark does not last for very long. Each bite should elicit a moan. 'Among the multitude of lovers, there was an outbreak of violent embraces...and impetuous hair pulling. After intercourse...the lower lip a little bit reddened from having repeatedly uttered moans of ecstasy'[*]—the phrase 'repeated moans' refers to the beloved enjoying the Gudka. The erotic texts say that this is the most pleasurable bite of all. When the kissing has become very passionate the lover deliberately changes tempo, merely contenting himself with rubbing the beloved's lower lip with his own for a couple of minutes before once again plunging in with the bite.

The next one is the *Impressed Bite* or *Uchunaka*. This is also made on the same spot (the middle of the lower lip) and is basically the same as the Gudka bite, but harder—hard enough

---

[*]Phyllis Granoff (ed.), *The Clever Adultress and Other Stories*, New Delhi: Motilal Banarasidass, 1993, p. 231.

Seema Anand

to leave a longer lasting bruise. It has no specific shape and is made by agitating the flesh between an upper tooth and the lower lip.

The *Bindu* or *Dot* is the tiniest bite, no larger than the size of a sesame seed and is done by nipping the skin between just two teeth. It was a favourite bite amongst lovers—not because it caused more excitement—but because it gave one status. The dot was such a specifically shaped bite that any kind of chip or unevenness of teeth would show up; only people with the very best teeth and expertise could make this mark to the exact size. Lovers who could make the Bindu were to be highly prized. The Bindu was made on the lower lip and on various other parts of the body as well.

After the Bindu came the *Bindu Mala* or *Necklace of Dots*. Here the lover made a series of sesame seed-shaped dots in little looping circles to look like a piece of jewellery. It was the bite of choice on long monsoon afternoons when the air was heavy with rain-soaked clouds chasing away the summer heat. Bindu necklaces were made on the neck, the curve of the waist and the thighs. As you can imagine, this kind of bite took a very long time, but for those who could do it, it was a badge of honour. In some regions of India, the dot necklace was also made to ornament the forehead and underarms, but this was a cultural preference, not everyone permitted this practice. According to the *Kama Sutra*, the women of North India did not like it at all.

The next two bites were the *Coral* and *Necklace of Corals*—*Pravalamani* and *Manimala*. These bites are called corals because they leave marks with distinctly red centres—like little pinpricks—but without drawing blood. The Coral is made when the same spot is squeezed several times between the top incisors and the lower lip. Sounds painful? And yet, much in demand because this was a sign of extreme attachment—you had to really care about someone to spend so much time and effort on them! It didn't need the mathematical expertise of the Bindu Mala, so it wasn't that much of a status symbol for the giver, more for the person receiving it because it showed that your lover was really into you. The Coral was primarily given on the left ear and the left cheek. It was a favourite of women when biting their lovers.

The Manimala, the necklace made of Coral Bites, was also made in curved or looping lines like the necklace of dots, but was concentrated more on the inside of the thighs, between the breasts or in a line towards the navel. This was a late afternoon bite.

'I am going away on a long journey and I am going to miss you'—the *Khandabhraka* or *Scattered Clouds Bite*. 'I have just returned from a long journey and have thought of nothing but a night of passion with you'—*Varaha-charvita* or *Chewing of the Wild Boar Bite*. These bites are made on the breasts and, says the *Kama Sutra*, are for people with fierce sexual energy. They are generally made in a state of great excitement, so there is no prescribed shape or size or tooth combination.

The Khandabhraka are small areas of scattered, irregular tooth marks. The Varaha-charvita is a wider area of irregular bites made close together. As the lover reaches the point of orgasm, he (or she) moves his head back and forth in unrestrained passion, so the bites look like long rows of tooth marks with red centres. The *Kama Sutra* says there is an artery that directly connects the nipples to the erotic nerve centre in the yoni (modern science confirms that the nipples are directly connected to the erotic nerve centre in the brain), and repeated and rhythmic love bites on the breasts will make the vulva spasm to give you the ultimate orgasm, breathless and all consuming.

But I promised you romance and romance you shall have.

Perhaps the most romantic of the love bites described in the *Kama Sutra* are bites that didn't have to be given directly to the lover but could be sent as 'messages' instead. You could place love bites on flower petals, exactly as you would mark them on her body, and send the petals to the beloved as a gift. Or you could send her leaves with bite marks—women used large flat leaves to apply make-up and traditionally a man would send these as gifts to the beloved, especially if he was requesting her company that evening.

And because each type of bite carried its own message, these love-bitten petals and leaves were like a carefully composed love letter.

The chapter on love bites ends with Vatsyayan reminding us that while bites are important for sexual arousal and satisfaction, for them to be arousing (rather than painful), they must be done with the right kind of pressure. If the beloved finds that the bites are too aggressive, she must tell the man to stop. And if he does not listen and lighten the pressure even after his beloved has asked him to, then Vatsyayan advises the woman to be twice as aggressive and bite him back twice as hard. If he has imprinted her with the Dot she must respond with a Necklace of Dots, if it is the Coral she should pay him back with a Necklace of Corals. If his head is resting on her breast she should bite him on the neck and, to indicate her annoyance, she is permitted to bite him with the Varaha-charvita (irregular bites with no specific shapes which are generally only made on the woman's breast).

If he still doesn't stop, Vatsyayan says she should grab him by the hair and, gluing her lips to his, she must force him to lie down and then, climbing on top of him, proceed to 'bite his whole body as though she was a mad woman'.

After a night of passion, when the woman sees her lover in

the midst of a group of friends, displaying the marks that she has made on him, she is secretly very pleased but will pretend to be very angry with him, accusing him of being unfaithful, insisting that some other woman has left these marks. She will toss her hair and leave the room, but only after she has secretly shown him her own love bites, which he has left on her. The *Kama Sutra* says that the love between two people who behave in this way, with passion as well as modesty, will never decrease, even after a hundred years.

My Advice

I do not recommend a public display of love bites—whatever the public acceptance of love bites may have been 2,000 years ago, showing off a neck full of bites no longer spells refinement, and as for bites on the cheeks, they are more likely to arouse police interest rather than anything erotic.

But love bites are important and exciting and should definitely be part of your erotic diet.

Try the hidden love bites. A few little private marks as a reminder of the previous night can do wonders for your sex life.

If it is romance you are looking for, then it is time to send bite marks on flowers. In a bouquet of ten flowers make sure that four are yellow in colour. On each yellow flower pick one petal and make three bite marks. Don't worry about the *Kama Sutra*'s message code—create your own bite symbols.

Attach a card with a 'bite' message—be creative with the message. Build your own erotic love bite vocabulary.

The next time you visit the dentist for teeth cleaning come back and make passionate love—let that be your special date. Weird? Perhaps, but the novelty factor will send your heart rate soaring.

Erotic Nerves

According to the ancient love texts, there are twenty-four nerves that run through the human body that cause erotic excitement. These nerves start in different parts of the body—for example, the eyes, cheeks, armpits, lower back—but they all eventually end up in the genitals. For men, the nerve endings are concentrated mostly in the anus, for women they are primarily in the vulva.

Aside from these twenty-four nerves women have another six major nerves of sexual excitement that run along the inside walls of the vulva, along different sides, ending at different depths. Which means that you can stimulate pretty much any point inside the vulva because each spot has the potential for orgasm—the possibilities are endless.

The Kama texts have an interesting way of categorizing erotic nerves. They are listed not by the areas where the nerves can be found but instead by their main method of arousal.

The first group of nerves mentioned are the ones that should be aroused with the mouth. According to Devadatta Shastri (one of the translators of the *Kama Sutra*), lips carry an electric charge. When you rub your lips on any part of the body for a length of time, the charge transfers itself to that nerve and it is this electric charge that causes excitement. Of the nerves that are to be excited by the mouth there are two in the eyes, two in the mouth, one in the lower lip, slightly left of centre, and one in the big toe of the left foot.

The best way to stimulate the eyes of the beloved is to alternately cover and uncover them while kissing them lightly and repeatedly. The left eye is most sensitive during the waning phase of the moon and the right eye during the waxing phase.

The two nerves inside the mouth are in the left cheek and should be aroused with the tongue. The tongue should be rolled so as to make a little point at the end and pushed against the inside of the cheek for maximum effect.

The nerve in the lip should be bitten—hard enough so that the lip becomes swollen but not so hard that it leaves a mark. If each bite draws a moan of pleasure from the beloved then you know it is working.

Finally, the nerve in the big toe—the last of the 'mouth' series. After having classified it as a 'mouth nerve' all the books, except one, change their mind and insist that the only way to stimulate this nerve is to play footsie with it. It was considered impure to place the foot in the mouth so the lover was advised to stimulate the toe with the toe. Only one ancient Tibetan text has continued to maintain that taking the toe into the mouth and sucking on it is the best way to stimulate it.

Toes were the most explicit symbol of sexual arousal (according to modern science, toes actually curl during orgasm). The curled big toe became one of the most delicately expressive metaphors of arousal in ancient India—the woman standing in front of her lover, gripped by desire and shyness, turns her foot slightly inwards and curls her big toe under it.[*]

Next, we have the nerves that are agitated by scratching. These nerves run through the ears, the forehead, thighs, hips, the navel, the lower back (the small of the back) and the bum. The nerves in the thighs, hips, lower back and bum have to be scratched quite aggressively; because they are set quite deep under the skin, they need heavy contact for stimulation. Of these, the deepest set nerves are the ones in the buttocks and it takes a great deal of effort to access them—you really have to knead that area with very sharp-edged nails to get to them.

One ancient text says that sitting down for too long can also press the buttock nerves and stimulate them. Before you get too excited—remember that furniture has changed since this was written. (Back then 'sitting down' would have meant on something hard and so there would have been a chance that these nerves could get activated—a soft sofa cushion would not have the same impact.) But in ancient times the fear of stimulating an erotic nerve by sitting for too long was such a serious concern that in the *Manusmriti* (also known as *The Laws of Manu*, the book on dharma by the sage Manu), the author suggests that the best way to protect young girls from their own sexual impulses is to get them to do housework of a very physical nature (where they cannot be sitting around on their bum) from as early as four years of age because this will keep their desires under control.

The last two 'nail' nerves run through the cartilage of the upper ear and across the forehead and could be aroused with both scratching and love bites—not because they were deep set and needed force but because this was a form of ornamentation,

---

[*]Sculptures at the Ajanta Caves too show a woman with head bent and eyes lowered as her toe curls under her.

it had to look like a necklace. Love bites and love scratches were left on the beloved as messages of passion. The *Kama Sutra* says one should stimulate the nerves in such a way that the beloved is left bejewelled with the marks of your passion.

Another two nerves run along the curve of the waist. These have to be stimulated by delicately nibbling on them with the love bite known as the Manimala or Necklace of Corals, mentioned earlier. The curve of the waist was perfumed with a very light fragrance that encouraged the lover to press his face deep into it and the bites were done in little looping necklaces of coral bites in this area while simultaneously kneading the bum, the hips and the thighs. It was believed that on rainy afternoons the nerves at the waist were the most sensitive of all.

All the erotic nerves pass through the navel on their way to the genitals, making it a very excitable spot. It is best excited by patting gently with an open palm but piercings, perfuming, massaging etc. are also considered effective. The great thing about the navel is that you can stimulate it very effectively yourself.

Saving the best for last—the 'open sesame' of all desire— the four erotic nerves that run through the nipples. There are two nerves in each nipple and these were considered the most vigorous in stimulating desire. Western science confirms that the nerves in the nipples are connected directly to the brain's erotic centre and carry the most powerful sexual impulses. In the sixth century BCE, Ayurveda had already told us that the nipple nerves hold the key to unlocking the yoni. The best way to stimulate the nipples is with chin stubble, the lips and the teeth. Placing your mouth and chin on the nipples, move your face from side to side very quickly, interspersing the movement with bites. If done right the woman will actually have the sensation of the muscles in her lower regions physically start to pulse and 'open up'—hence the nickname 'open sesame'.

Aside from these twenty-four nerves that carry arousal across the body, the vulva has its own collection of in-house erotic nerves. Six in number, the brilliant thing about them is that they run along different walls of the yoni, and at different depths, which means that penises of all sizes and shapes—long, short, thick, thin, crooked, straight, bent—can hit some point of excitement or the other. If you can't find the elusive G-spot, don't worry, the entire passage is virtually popping with X, Y and Z spots.

The six nerves in the yoni are called Sati, Asati, Subhaga, Durbhaga, Putrini and Duhitrini.

At the entrance of the yoni, to the right and left of the clitoris respectively, sit the Subhaga and the Durbhaga nerves. According to the *Kama Sutra*, if you stimulate the Subhaga the woman starts to feel happy and calm—it makes her skin glow, her face look more beautiful and her limbs feel light. The Durbhaga is like the alter ego of the Subhaga, and if stimulated during the waxing phase of the moon, it will make the woman angry and 'dry'—both in looks and temperament: the voice becomes harsh, the complexion becomes yellow and dull and all the problems of old age, like joint pains and hair loss, start to befall the woman. However, during the waning phase this does not happen.

At the very top of the passage, just before the entrance to the uterus, are the Putrini and Duhitrini nerves, which are massaged to enable pregnancy.

Somewhere in the middle of the yoni are the Sati and Asati. These two nerves seem to be far more complex because their stimulation is based on individual characteristics. If a woman who is of a calm, introverted and chaste temperament has her Asati stimulated, she becomes very excitable and begins to act like a 'loose' and 'wanton' woman. If a woman who is fiery, extroverted and fond of male attention has her Sati rubbed, she becomes 'short of breath, listless, ill and loses her desire to practice the sixty-four arts of pleasure'. It is very important to properly understand the temperament of the woman before you decide how to arouse her.

The Sati nerve can be massaged heavily to cause abortion or as a contraceptive.[*]

The love texts say that these nerves can also be aroused from the outside, but there is very little agreement on the points of arousal. One source says that pressing and kneading the curve of the waist and the sides of the hips will excite the Asati nerve, and moving around the circle of the waist with kisses will get the Durbhaga going. Kneading, scratching and kissing the buttocks and lower back will cause both the Subhaga and Duhitrini to flare up and kissing on the mouth brings the Putrini into play.

Another source says the arousal point for Sati is in the breasts—the breasts should be kneaded and pressed heavily. Asati can be excited by scratching the armpit, Subhaga is in the upper lip and needs to be kissed and bitten and Durbhaga reacts to being alternately stroked and struck on the hips. The Putrini nerve is up in the cheeks, which should be kissed and sucked and, finally, the Duhitrini, which sits in the buttocks, has to be stroked, struck and bitten.

But, says the *Kama Sutra*, if you are in the throes of passion and are finding it difficult to locate precise spots, just focus on the hairless areas. The erotic nerves run through the whole body, so you could potentially excite them at any point, but the best spots for stimulation are where there is no hair. Some parts are

---

[*]Alain Danielou (trans), *The Complete Kama Sutra*, New York: Simon and Schuster, 1993.

naturally hairless like the lips, eyes, toes, etc. Other parts were depilated (waxed, shaved). Men and women were advised to remove their pubic hair from the roots regularly—the Brazilian wax is not a modern-day invention.

There was a strictly prescribed schedule of hair removal for men—beard hair was to be trimmed every fourth day, armpit hair removed every fifth day, pubic hair shaved every fifth day and removed from the roots every tenth day, and so on. Women removed body hair every day. Interesting fact—back then it was believed that the armpit was the mirror image of the yoni. If a woman had no hair in her armpits then her vagina would be hairless too.

Moles were also significant. If the woman had a mole on her cheek then she would have a mole on her yoni as well, either on the outer lips of the yoni or inside. Moles on the yoni, known as yoni prashansak (that which makes the vagina delightful), were very desirable. Because they were thought to indicate the exact point where the erotic nerve finished, they made the lover's job very easy. You didn't have to go hunting around for the correct spot to excite.

Men loved women with moles (beauty spots) on the face. Women would draw moles on the face and on the yoni as part of their shringhar. In India, the facial mole is still an indication of sexiness—but now you know why!

Aside from kisses, love bites, scratches and various other physical means, there was also the tradition of using mantras or sound vibrations to excite the erotic nerves.

In India, there is an ancient tradition of using mantras to augment any kind of physical action—sound vibrations energize the cells so that all actions become more effective. This was the case in lovemaking too. You stimulate the nerves all over the body by the usual means (scratching, biting, kissing etc.) and then you energize the nerve endings (in the clitoris or vulva) with sound vibrations so that they become totally receptive.

They say that Kamadeva's five arrows—with which he conquers lovers—are made of flowers strung on mantras. Different sounds create different effects, so mantras are made of an assortment of syllables, sounds, pitches and tempos. For instance, Kamadeva's arrows are created from the syllables A, E, I, O and U and each arrow has its own target. The sound of 'A' pierces the heart, 'E' is for the forehead, 'I' is aimed at the breast, 'O' is for the vagina and the target for 'U' is the eyes.

There are other more complex mantras made up of a series of syllables.

'Han-k-sh-yam' was the mantra for protecting your wife's chastity if you were going away for an extended period of time. The man chanted the mantra and then placed its energy at the opening of the vulva. This diverted the erotic sensation and ensured that she would not fall into the trap of any other man in his absence.

The most powerful syllable is 'bli'—it is known as the rays of the morning sun. Just as the appearance of the sun's rays propels the entire earth into work mode, this mantra can propel all dormant erotic nerves and spots into full arousal. This mantra is meant to be placed in the very centre of the yoni. It is so powerful that if any man places it in a woman for seven consecutive days, she will become his slave forever more. Even when she goes to the land of Yamaraj (the land of the dead) where all earthly memories are wiped clean, she will still not be able to forget this arousal and in death, too, she will remain the man's slave.

The placing of mantras and sound vibrations is as complicated as it sounds. But the physical stimulation of erotic nerves and G-spots is simpler and a lot more fun, so perhaps focus on that.

My Advice

The *Kama Sutra* says that before you begin making love 'Kama, the God of Love, must be invoked and installed in every part of the body'—then, and only then, must sex be performed.

I think that is what your goal should be—to help invoke the God of Love and plant him in your lover's body, arouse them so that they feel every nerve tingling in anticipation.

The chapter on erotic nerves is great but it is not gospel, there are no hard and fast rules; it is simply a model, a set of suggestions that you can use according to what best suits you. Everything in the *Kama Sutra* comes with several possibilities, giving you the chance to pick things that you like as well as the opportunity of trying something new.

Think of which nerves you want to experiment with. They are not all easy to follow but start with something that both of you like and gradually move on to things outside your comfort zone. Remember that both men and women have erotic nerves, so be generous in your loving. It can be very seductive to give rather than receive.

And the most stimulating quality is intellect—stimulate each other's minds. Humour is sexy—don't get serious about all of it. For instance, most people cannot at all fathom how to place a mantra in the yoni. Well—you don't have to do it seriously. Remember you are using this book as a modern-day guide to the arts of seduction; it has to be adapted to suit your needs. Why not make a shared joke out of it, something to do on special occasions? Let it be your own little sexy activity— you will be surprised at how much pleasure and arousal there is in shared laughter.

One of my favourites bits in this chapter is the little nugget about moles—the idea that if there is one on the cheek it has its twin on the genitals. Turn it into a game of foreplay. Make it a secret message. The next time you want to seduce your partner show up at the dinner table with a mole painted on—they will know what is on your mind. Draw another mole somewhere else on your body—make it a sexy treasure hunt.

Sex should be joyous, full of fun and games and filled with laughter. If that is not how it is for you, you need to spend more time on it, take it slower, try something new and, most importantly, *believe* that as a human being you were created to enjoy it!

The Phases of the Moon

'By following the Chandrakalas (lunar calendar) and varying the site of your caresses accordingly you will see your lover light up in successive places, like a figure cut in moonstone when the moon strikes on it....'[*]

The *Kama Sutra* says that the different phases of the moon create different erogenous zones all around our body which shift and change every day—each phase has its own corresponding G-spot and each G-spot has its own method of arousal. Chandrakalas—the art of seduction based on the changing phases of the moon—explains where these sensitive spots are located on any given night, where best to stimulate your lover and how.

Legend has it that the Chandrakalas were written by a sage named Bhabravya in the fourth century BCE. His theory was that every night, with each phase of the moon, a different part of the body becomes more sensitive, and if those areas were to be excited with specific types of contact—kissing, biting, scratching—you could bring your lover to full arousal every single time.

---

[*]Alex Comfort, *The Koka Shastra: Being the Ratirahasya of Kokkoka and Other Medieval Indian Writings on Love*, London: G. Allen and Unwin, 1964, p. 107.

In his extensive treatise, Bhabravya took into account the power and the pull of the moon in all its permutations and combinations—how the effect of the moon changes according to the seasons and how it shifts as the night progresses. The night is divided into four quarters and with each quarter the moon is closer to or further from the surface of the earth, so its effect on the erogenous zones changes. He explained how the moon affects people of different physical characteristics and temperaments in different ways—who gets excited at what time and needs to be stimulated at what spot. It was an incredible piece of writing.

Unfortunately the text has not survived, not even a small part of it. The only information we have of this work is what other authors have translated and quoted over the centuries, and so our knowledge of it is quite fragmented and at times contradictory—but I think it is all useful, in some way or the other.

I have transcribed some of it for you. Have a go—you never know which one will work and you'll have a lot of fun trying it out. Even if you don't actually hit an erogenous zone, it will add a whole new dimension of romance and novelty to your lovemaking.

The Chandrakalas were written for both men and women. The erogenous zones in both men and women are identical but on opposite sides of the body. There are thirty erogenous zones on the body corresponding to the thirty phases of the moon's cycle, fifteen on the left and fifteen on the right. The seat of sexual excitement sits in the hair parting at the top of the head. Starting on the new moon with the big toe—of the left foot for women and the right foot for men—sexual excitement moves up the body for the fifteen days of the waxing half of the month until it reaches the head during the full moon and then starts back down again on the opposite side of the body for the next fifteen nights (of the waning half) until it reaches the foot once again.

Most of the translations focus more on women because their arousal was considered more important. Men, we are told, have the advantage of being more visual. When they see their lovers come to arousal, it excites them and when they see that this arousal is a result of their own actions, it increases their own excitement and pleasure.

Here is a list of the most basic spots and their stimuli.

Beginning on the first day after the full moon, which corresponds to the sixteenth phase of the moon, the woman's head and hair have the greatest sexual energy and should be kissed and massaged gently in order to fully excite the woman.

On the second day (seventeenth phase), it is the eyes that are most sensitive and should be kissed repeatedly—the right eye is more sensitive during the waxing phase of the moon, the left one during the waning phase.

On the third day (eighteenth phase), you must focus on the lips. We are told they should be kissed and softly bitten. The lower lip in particular should be repeatedly bitten, enough to make it swollen, but not enough to leave a lasting mark. Each bite should draw a soft moan from your lover—that shows it has hit the spot.

On the fourth day (nineteenth phase), it is the cheeks. The cheeks should also be kissed and softly bitten. Did you know that according to the *Kama Sutra*, the cheeks are amongst the most sensitive and erotic parts of the body and their nerve endings are exactly like the nerves in the vulva?

The fifth day (twentieth phase), particularly the fifth day of the waning moon, is the day of rest for the man. It is known as the lazy man's day because on the fifth day a woman's sexuality is self-sufficient and she does not require a man's help to achieve arousal.

On the sixth day (twenty-first phase), the throat is most sensitive and it should be very gently scratched with the nails.

On the seventh day (twenty-second phase), it is the side of the waist. For this also, gentle scratching is best.

On the eighth day (twenty-third phase), it is the nipples that are most sensitive.

On the ninth day (twenty-fourth phase), the entire bosom area—the breasts, the nipples, the cleavage and the area under the breasts are waiting for attention.

On the tenth day (twenty-fifth phase), the navel is most excitable. The best way to stimulate the navel is by tapping it gently with an open palm.

On the eleventh day (twenty-sixth phase), it is the buttocks. The buttocks should be kneaded with the nails and squeezed and pressed hard.

On the twelfth day (twenty-seventh phase), the woman's knees are most sensitive and the best way to stimulate them is by pressing against them with your own knees.

On the thirteenth day (twenty-eighth phase), some say it is when the calves that need attention, others feel it is the ankle that is more sensitive at this time. Biting and scratching are recommended, but kissing works best. If it is the ankle, then pressing it with one's own ankle is recommended.

On the fourteenth day (twenty-ninth phase), it is the foot that should be gently pressed with your own foot.

On the fifteenth day (thirtieth phase), there is a slight disagreement on whether the most sensitive point is the big toe of the left foot (we are going down the left side) or whether it should be the left thumb (the base of the thumb). My advice would be: don't waste time choosing. Give them both equal amounts of attention.

This is just the basic list. Now let's get specific.

Suppose you were making love in the second quarter of the night. This is supposed to be the time of the strongest sexual desires in women—the pull of the moon is such that any woman would be unquenchable at this time. The way to deal with this is to increase the amount of pressure with which you touch your lover. So if something needs to be pressed you need to press it harder, if a spot needs kissing you need to shift from using the lips to the teeth, stroking becomes squeezing, and so on.

Below is the same table of erogenous zones, the difference is how to stimulate them for stronger sexual excitement—it's time to up the passion!

Big toes—the big toe should be pressed with your own toe. If her toes are curled, flatten them out, if necessary, apply pressure. If you are pressing her toe from above, then the pressing action should be like a pulse—up, down, up, down. If you are touching her toe from underneath, rub it from side to side with the back of your own toe.

Feet—there is some disagreement on this. Feet are very important because of the number of nerve endings in that area. Some authors feel it is enough to press your lover's feet with your own, just increase pressure. Others feel that in the second quarter, the pressure applied should be stronger—so the foot should be struck with your own foot. And there is also one who says that this calls for a complete change of technique—proceed by kissing the foot and nibbling on it.

Ankles—again most of the suggestions are to press with one's own ankle, except for one voice that says it is better to kiss the ankle. But I think it would depend on the position that you are in at the time.

Knees—it is best to press your lover's knees with your own. Press harder. But—this is extremely important—knees should only be stimulated if you are both in the exact same position, either standing, lying down side by side facing each other or lying on top of each other.

Navel—the navel should only be gently patted with the open palm, but you can use the forefinger and trace circles around the navel and at this time, you can apply more pressure.

The chest area—knead and stroke hard with a balled up fist. This area should be patted and stroked.

Breasts—pressing, patting, fondling, squeezing with pressure. This is a very versatile area and one that is equally exciting for both men and women.

Armpits—everyone is in agreement that the armpit should be scraped with the nails. This is an area that is generally ignored these days but in the time of the *Kama Sutra* it seems to have been one of the key areas of the body for erotic sensations. This unlikely spot was also a mirror of the vulva—as I mentioned earlier, experts said that a hairless armpit indicated a hairless vagina. The *Kama Sutra* tells us that in certain regions, people thought the armpit was the most exciting place to kiss.

Neck—the suggestion again is to scrape gently with nails. Interestingly, in the Chandrakalas, the neck does not enjoy a position of any particular importance as an erotic spot. It's just an also-ran. As the moon goes into the second quarter and erotic desires run very high, it seems as though nothing changes very drastically with the neck. Personally, I disagree. There's nothing quite as fabulous as the neck for erogenous sensations.

Cheeks—sexual energies really explode when it comes to the cheeks. The *Kama Sutra* says that cheeks should be adorned with love bites, scraped with nails or kissed very vigorously. One of the main erotic nerves begins at the cheek and ends in the vulva. If the lover had a little black mole on her cheek (especially the left cheek), then it was believed that she would have one on her vagina as well—all the more exciting because you could 'see' it.

Lips—the lips are to be squeezed, bitten and kissed, as before but much harder.

Eyes and eyelids—press with the palms and kiss alternately.

Forehead—unlike other spots, this is one area that is calmer during the second quarter of the night. The best way to deal with the forehead at this time is to kiss it gently.

Head—this is the time to twist your lover's hair around your fingers and pull—the harder the better.

The hair parting—at this time of the night, the hair parting should be scraped and scratched with the nails.

Waist—scratch and kiss.

Thighs—press with the thighs. Love bites are also recommended.

The *Rati Manjari* by Jayadeva, one of several ancient Indian erotic texts, adds that when the erogenous zones shift from the left to the right side of the body, you should celebrate this change by inverting the position of lovemaking—let the woman take her position on top. But the author adds the caveat—'only if the woman is strong'—because being on top was hard work.

The *Dinalapanika Sukasaptati* (*The Seventy Discourses of the Parrot*) says that the Chandrakalas should be synchronized with the start of the menstrual cycle, not the lunar cycle.

Nandikesvara, one of the authors of whose work forms a part of the *Ratirahasya* (also known as the *Koka Shastra*), says that biting, kissing, scratching etc. should be accompanied by sound vibrations or mantras (see chapter Erotic Nerves). So each erogenous spot should be stimulated with a physical action and also by sound.

The most complete account of the Chandrakalas is given by Gonikaputra (another author whose work Kokkoka, the poet, relied greatly on in compiling the *Koka Shastra*)[*] and is based on the moon being in the last quarter of the night; in other words it is for women who enjoy sex at the end of the night and in the very early hours of dawn. Interestingly, Western science believes that this is the time when our bodies are at their 'most sexual' and for those of us who can manage to wake up at 6 a.m., it can lead to the most rewarding sex.

But Gonikaputra takes a very different approach from the others—he says that with each shifting phase it is not just one spot that becomes excited every day—rather, it is a combination of spots. So his table of erogenous zones has several activities for each day. He also seems to have ignored the feet and toes completely in his ranking and focused much more on the armpits and nipples instead. So even though he begins by saying that on the first day, the sexual excitement begins at the lowermost part of the body, the places he suggests for kissing are nowhere near the feet, they are all in the upper half of the body. But I think you should try it anyway—trust me, you will not be disappointed.

The concept of the Chandrakalas was a very popular one and certainly the *Kama Sutra* gave them a place of great importance in the arts of seduction. But equally there are those who dismiss the entire theory as a piece of fantasy with no basis in fact whatsoever.

Whether this it is science or fantasy, I think the main purpose of the Chandrakalas was to add variety to sex. The

---

[*]See Alex Comfort (trans.), *The Koka Shastra, Being the Ratirahasya of Kokkoka, and Other Medieval Indian Writings on Love,* London: George Allen and Unwin, 1964.

Kama Sutra maintains that for sex to be exciting and fulfilling, nothing should be repetitive.

Yes, there are some areas of the body that are always exciting to caress regardless of the shifting phases of the moon. The idea of aligning erogenous zones with the lunar calendar just means there are other areas to arouse.

My Advice

If you would like to try out the Chandrakalas, get yourself an app that tells you what phase of the moon you are in. Once you are able to figure out the phase of the moon, pick the simplest routine and work with it. Don't worry about the combinations—the very fact of trying something new will add enough novelty to your lovemaking to keep you going for a while.

The fun (or chaos) of using the Chandrakalas should lessen your inhibitions—it will become more like a game and will remove your embarrassment in exploring your lover's body more openly.

Don't do it every day—anything you do every day becomes boring and stops being fun. Pick something from the charts that you like the sound of and then work out the day on which it should be practised. Make a date with your partner for that night, tell them what you have in mind and give each other the time to get excited about it.

Don't be pedantic. Remember our skin is a giant erogenous zone—everything you do can be a turn-on—it just depends on how you do it. As the author of *Passion Play: Ancient Secrets for a Lifetime of Health and Happiness Through Sensational Sex*, Felice Dunas, says: the most tantalizing are the tiniest of touches—'the most delicate brushing of a hair, the slow progress of fingertips or nails or tongue across the skin, the slightest change or pause.' Do it slowly, deliberately—linger on the moment, make your partner wonder what you will do next.

The more subtle the movements the sharper the senses become, so that the tiniest change in pressure or movement is noticeable. And it is not just exciting for the partner on the receiving end but equally erotic to know that you are having this effect on your beloved.

If you really want to become 'the best lover', begin with investing time in understanding what turns your partner on. Create a table of your own erogenous zones. You will be surprised to see how much of the human body is sexually responsive.

Scratching in the Art of Lovemaking

According to the *Kama Sutra*, scratching was one of the top three must-have skills for any lover. Scratches were not just random marks of passion made in the heat of the moment. Much like love bites, they had a vocabulary all of their own— different types of scratches on specific spots carried different messages. According to the *Kama Sutra*, a scratch was like a love letter, and like a love letter it had the power to excite you each time you looked at it. Just as you would pick up a love letter and read and reread it, hold it close to your heart, sigh over the words your lover had penned down, similarly the scratches spoke to you in the voice of your lover. In *The Satasai*, the medieval romantic poet Bihari writes of his young heroine who will not allow her scratch marks to heal. Her lover has gone off on a journey but left love wounds on her— four long scratches on her upper thigh that say he will miss her. These marks are all she has of him to keep her company during the long lonely nights and she is determined to hold on to them. Each time they begin to scab over, she digs them up with her own nails—because that's where he had said he would be thinking of her.

According to the *Kama Sutra*, the sight of love scratches, even on a total stranger, was enough to fire up all of one's lust and passion. If a man, walking down the road perchance sees a woman wearing the marks of love, be he a man of firm resolve and pure mind, he will feel aroused and find himself desiring the woman, even if she is a total stranger, and he will go out of his way to try and make the acquaintance of that woman.

Similarly, if a woman sees the man marked with love scratches, no matter how modest, chaste or faithful she may be, she will find herself wanting to make love to him, she will not be able to help herself.

And scratches weren't just something that excited you in the heat of passion, they were equally effective the morning after—or even several mornings after. The *Kama Sutra* says that when a woman sees the marks of her lover's nails on the concealed parts of her body, by the sight of them her passion for him is aroused again, even if it has been dying a slow death over the past few days.

The expert lover knew exactly how to scratch, when to lightly scrape the nails across the skin to leave the beloved quivering in anticipation and when to really drive in the nails to heighten the ecstasy of the moment. Vatsyayan says if you can learn this art you will be counted among the most desirable of lovers and will never have to suffer through average sex again.

Now that's a big claim!

So let the lessons begin.

Both men and women scratched.

Love scratches were made to be seen. As I've mentioned, in this period of court romances, public marks of love were like badges of honour—they were the sign of a good lover, a means to show off your sexual prowess in bed and they were worn like ornaments.

And just as only people with good teeth were 'allowed' to leave love bites, only people with good nails were allowed to make scratch marks. 'Good nails' were shiny and even, with no bumps and ridges, they had to all be of equal length—not broken or chipped. They had to be strong so they wouldn't crack while kneading or pushing and they had to be clean and smooth with no dirt stuck underneath.

For men especially, the difference between good nails and bad nails could be the difference between getting the woman or not. The *Kama Sutra* says that women of Gauda (North Bengal) were particularly attracted to men with good nails.

Love scratching was done with the nails of the left hand—the right hand was used for eating, the left hand was used for sex and cleaning yourself.

The nails of the left hand were shaped according to your sexual energy and your proficiency in bed. If you had 'fierce sexual energy' you shaped your nails into two or three points, like the teeth of a saw; if you were of medium energy you filed them into a single point, like the beak of a parrot; and if you were of mild sexual energy you shaped your nails flat, in the shape of a half moon.

The *Kama Sutra* tells us that the people of South India have naturally perfect nails for scratching—strong, resilient nails that can take a lot of pushing and kneading. The people of Maharashtra are of such high sexual energy that they keep the nails of both hands shaped for love scratching.

Love scratches, says the *Kama Sutra,* should be made on seven specific areas of the body—the neck, cheeks, breasts (chest), back, thighs (inner thigh and crotch, as well as outer thighs and the length of the leg), lower belly and buttocks. As we've seen, these spots are erogenous zones with major erotic nerves running through them. Some texts include an eighth spot—the armpits—as one of the most popular spots for making love scratches.

Vatsyayan acknowledges that in the throes of passion it is not possible to remember all the rules and lovers do tend to scratch anywhere they want, but one should try one's best to remember. Although every part of the body can potentially be an erogenous zone, some areas just shouldn't be forcibly aroused.

It's a tricky situation. If the right places are not fully excited it can lead to terribly dissatisfying sex and can make the woman feel ill with frustration. If the wrong places are over-excited it can lead to a negative reaction that can cause her to faint.

So in order to protect your lover's mental and physical health it was best to know exactly which spots to scratch.

But if you truly cannot stick to the rules the author offers one helpful hint—when passions are running high and orgasm is approaching, kiss her all over her body and when you see her eyes roll, that is an indication of where her excitement lies at that moment—that's the spot to concentrate your energies.

When to scratch?

Love scratching is not something that you do at the beginning of foreplay—it is for when excitement has mounted and passions are hot. Vatsyayan says that if you begin scratching your lover in the very early stages of foreplay, far from being exciting it is merely annoying and can lead to things coming to an untimely end.

Also not every sexual encounter is suitable for scratching. It had to be for specific occasions.

For instance, the most popular occasion for love scratches was the eve of a long journey. Not only would this be an extra-long night of very passionate lovemaking, driven as it was by the heartbreak of impending separation, it was also the time to leave your mark on the beloved, something to remember you by. Traditionally, the mark on this occasion was four short straight scratches on the upper thigh that said 'I'm your lover, wait for me to return.'

Another occasion was the return of the lover from a long journey. When the lover came back after an extended period of time, the beloved would greet him with mock crossness (narazgi or roothna—words that are hard to translate. It means a sort of mock anger that the lover is invited to wipe away with kisses and lovemaking). On this occasion one would leave five curved scratches on the breast of the beloved (man or woman) to say 'we have made love and now finally I can sleep in peace again.'

Love scratches were also used for the first lovemaking after the woman finished her period.

But my favourite—love scratches could also be used to fake an orgasm. Just because it was the era of the *Kama Sutra* doesn't mean there was an infallible formula for satisfaction—lovers in ancient India too had to fake it sometimes.

So, if you had the reputation for being a passionate lover but were really not feeling the heat on a particular night and yet you could not let the world know that you were in a slump (it was a kiss-and-tell society)—scratch!

If you were losing interest in your beloved, but didn't want them to know—scratch!

If you were an indifferent lover but on your travels (where people didn't know you), you wanted to tell a good story about yourself—you'd shape your nails like the teeth of a saw and scratch!

Types of Scratches

In the heat of passion the *Kama Sutra* may forgive you for scratching wherever you want but the type of scratch still had to conform to standards. Scratch marks were displayed and if you got the love marks wrong it would brand you as a bad lover—and that, as Vatsyayan repeatedly tells us, is a fate worse than death. So pay attention.

The first type of scratch is to arouse desperate cravings but not satisfy any. Scrape the nail across the flesh, barely touching the skin, just enough to give your lover goose flesh and get their nerves tingling. You can do this either with all the five nails or just the thumbnail. This should not leave any marks. The best place for this is the lower lip, the cheeks and the breasts. According to Yashodhara (the most famous commentator of the *Kama Sutra* from the thirteenth century), the Bengalis are the best at this—they do not scratch with their nails, they just touch.

All other scratches are harder and will leave marks. For these the skin has to first be prepared. This is done by alternately pulling the skin gently and pinching it fairly hard. It sounds complicated but Vatsyayan says it is just a matter of practice.

There are eight different types of love scratches.

Acchurita or *Knife Stroke*—this one is known for the clicking sound it makes when the thumbnail strikes the other nails. Press your thumbnail into the flesh first and then bring the other nails down hard next to it, making the 'click' sound as they come together. This can be done on all the recommended scratch points according to your pleasure.

Ardhachandra or *Half-moon*—this looks like a semi-circle and is made on the neck or below the breasts with just one nail (any nail) at a time. When done with the middle finger it leaves the most permanent mark, but when done with the little finger it is most effective in arousing excitement. You can leave a series

Seema Anand

of these marks to look like a necklace of Ardhachandras.

Mandala or *Circle*—two half-moon marks are made facing each other. The best spots for the Mandala are the lower belly, the inner thigh and the bottom.

Rekha or *Dash*—a scratch in the shape of a straight line. This can be made anywhere on the recommended spots. The only proviso is that it has to be short, about the length of two or three thumb breadths.

Vyaghranakha or *Tiger's Claw*—this is a curving mark made with the nails of the thumb and the first three fingers of the hand (not using the little finger). The Vyaghranakha is made on the face and breasts. Normally it would just be one mark, but if more than one are made, they are placed one behind the other.

Mayurpadaka or *Peacock's Foot*—when the nipple is seized by all five nails and pulled outwards, the nail marks around the breast are known as the Mayurpadaka.

Shashaplutaka or *Hare's Jump*—if the beloved has shown with the rolling of her eyes and her moans that she has enjoyed the Mayurpadaka, then the lover is advised to pull the nipple harder. The marks left by this added force are called the Shashaplutaka.

Utpalapattraka or *Lotus Leaf*—these marks do not have a distinct shape but tend to look a bit like an open lotus leaf. They are made on the side of the breasts or the buttocks by digging in and pinching hard with all the nails.

These are the suggested nail marks but of course there can be many variations—as many variations as there are lovers and nights of love. Everyone can scratch during the frenzied moments of passion—only the skilled lover will understand how to turn the frenzy into an art form.

Love scratches had an interesting vocabulary. They were the manifestation of Memory, which is another name for Kamadeva—sometimes he makes you remember and sometimes he makes you forget, and each state brings its own pleasure and sorrow. Love scratches were meant to remind you of the qualities of the beloved—beauty, youth, what you did together, and so on.

Four short straight lines on the upper thigh brought painful memories because that meant the lover had gone away on a long journey, but they were also agonizingly pleasurable because they reminded you of your last night together.

The Peacock's Foot on the breast was intoxicating in its arousal—it was made during orgasm when the lover returned. Looking at it took the beloved back to her orgasm each time.

Love scratches were the tell-tale mark of infidelity. Many a heart was broken at the sight of illicit scratch marks on the body of the husband or the lover. Sanskrit poetry is full of verses written on the illicit scratch mark:

> You didn't go the scoundrel's house,
> You went to the woods, didn't you?
> How else could you have gotten that garland
> Of flame-tree flowers you're wearing?[*]

The garland of 'flame-tree flowers' refers to the necklace of red scratch marks around the neck. The heroine had employed a maid to carry a message to her lover, but when she sees

---

[*]*Bouquet of Rasa and River of Rasa by Bhanudatta Misra, edited and translated by Sheldon Pollock*, New York: New York University Press, 2009, p. 33.

her coming back with the love scratches, she realizes that the wretch has managed to seduce the man for herself.

The *Kama Sutra* also has a list of when *not* to leave scratch marks.

Do not leave love scratches on someone else's spouse as this could lead to a great deal of trouble in a relationship.

Similarly, on an unmarried girl—unless you plan to marry her—you must not leave love scratches that can be seen by everyone, as that will ruin her reputation. If you really wanted to leave a scratch mark then it should be done on a hidden part of the body where the beloved can enjoy it without being discovered.

If you were not able to be with your beloved you could 'send' scratch marks to the beloved as a parcel. The parcel consisted of a red wax seal—the kind used to seal letters. The red wax was pressed with a coin to create the desired shape and into this the nail marks were embedded. This seal indicated an intense erotic longing—'I am dreaming of making love to you'. If tied with a red thread it meant, 'my passion for you has reached its height' and when embedded with five nail marks it implied, 'I have been pierced by the five arrows of Kamadeva'.

A man or a woman with absolutely no love scratches was an object of great pity—obviously there was no love in their life and hadn't been in a very long time!

When passions have been given up long ago
Love may disappear
Unless there are wounds made by nails
To prompt memories of the abode of passion.[*]

---

[*]Wendy Doniger and Sudhir Kakar, *Kama Sutra*, New York: Oxford University Press, 2009, p. 47.

My Advice

Put aside all the instructions for a moment and focus on the pleasure of it—scratching and being scratched is orgasmic and a natural instinct of sexual arousal.

Unlike the lovers of the *Kama Sutra*, in modern times scratching seems to almost exclusively be the role of the woman—she scratches, he receives. And, again, unlike the *Kama Sutra*, today scratches seem to be restricted only to the back and occasionally the shoulders. But it works! If he can get her to unbearable excitement she will automatically scratch him—it's a sort of release valve. When she scratches him it stimulates certain pleasure points in his back, making him come even harder.

The romance is in the position. To hold your lover tight in your arms and scratch their back means that you are embracing face to face—the *Kama Sutra* says this is the most intimate position because it is the position of the cuddle, the position that makes one feel most loved and cherished.

But scratching can also be a sexy shared moment even if you are not having sex. To slip your hands under your lover's clothes and feel their back, momentarily, briefly, no matter where you are, and just scrape gently with the nails creates a frisson that very few other things can.

But what about flirtation? Scratching has great currency for sexual arousal and orgasms but can it be used to start a flirtation? Is it an art of seduction?

This is where the *Kama Sutra*'s suggestion comes in—to send love scratches as a message to the beloved. Imagine being able to pack all that sexual arousal, all the excitement, all the suggestiveness of the scratch into a little message. Now imagine the potential for flirtation.

Get creative. You can send scratches via emoticons, cards,

text messages with nail shaped scratch marks. They will definitely get his or her attention.

Send a photo of your most recent manicure—it'll keep the flirtation light-hearted and fun.

This is an excellent way to excite and entice but still stay mysterious. It hints at the intimacy of scratching and everything that goes with it without being explicit.

The *Kama Sutra* stresses that it is all about rasa or the mood—your actions must be geared to create the right mood. The playful suggestiveness of a 'scratch-package' will create the mood of anticipation, of possibilities, of mystery.

The Art of the Curved Finger

In eighteenth-century Europe it was a disease, in the nineteenth century it was the cure.

In eighteenth-century Europe, using the fingers to pleasure yourself was a crime and could have you burnt at the stake—it was a disease that had to be stamped out. By the nineteenth century, women were diagnosed to be suffering from an unreasonable illness called 'hysteria' and the fingers became a cure. You could relieve a woman of most of her symptoms (the common cold was not included, unfortunately) by stimulating her with the fingers until she reached her orgasm. Most doctors offered this service, at the regular fee of two dollars a sitting, and it was a most effective cure. The only problem being it was terribly slow! It could take as much as an hour to stimulate the woman properly—a problem that would be solved some years later with the advent of the mechanized vibrator (more of which in the chapter Dildos—Romance, Seduction, Fulfilment).

Two thousand years ago, however, the *Kama Sutra* believed that the art of the curved finger was the ultimate way to pleasure a woman, it was the doorway to orgasm. According to

Ayurveda, the yoni (vulva) is a veritable Aladdin's cave, full of G-spots—erogenous points that are located on all sides and at different depths. And only the curved finger could do justice to them—the soft finger-tipped massage alternating with the gently grazing nail—it was the key to mind-blowing orgasms and ecstasy.

Ayurveda explains that each finger of the hand represents a different element. From the thumb to the little finger each holds the energies of fire (agni), air (vayu), space (aakash), earth (prithvi) and water (jal) respectively. So each finger will have a different impact when used. If you combine two or more fingers the energies change accordingly. The reaction of each erogenous point when massaged or scraped with a specific combination of fingers will be different. If you press slightly to the north or the south of the point, even that will change the reaction—the combinations are endless.

The finger combinations are known as mudras and each one is different.

Some can make the woman melt into orgasm, some will agitate her into a quivering mass of anticipation, some can make her calm and deep like a pool of honey while others will flare her up like burnt chillies.

Try them all to see which will do what.

Karana—this is the index finger on its own. The ancient love texts say that the index finger should not be used on its own. The index finger is the energy of vayu (air) which, according to Vedic science, is the manifestation of the universe. Everything begins and ends with vayu—everything is born from it and, in the end, everything will be absorbed into it. And so this finger is too powerful to be used by itself, the burst of energy will numb the excitement instead of generating it.

Kanak—with the middle finger sitting on top of the index finger, massage and scrape gently with the nails. This is an excellent mudra for the start of sex. Part the lips of the yoni and gradually insert the two fingers, but only as far as the clitoris. Twist the hand back and forth, get everything moving.

Vikan—this is the same as the Kanak but with reversed fingers, so the index finger sits on the middle finger. Notice this changes both the width and the length of the mudra. It can now be used to go further into the vulva. This is great for building up excitement.

Kankara—this mudra uses the second, third and little fingers while keeping the thumb and index finger closed. With this combination you penetrate through to the deepest point in the vulva. This calms the itch that nothing else can ever reach.

Kamayudh—the middle and little fingers joined to the thumb create the shape of Kamadeva's bow. This is also good for widening and loosening the yoni.

Kamausadh—join the little and middle fingers to resemble the crescent moon. The crescent moon is the most effective way to reach the erogenous points on the 'ceiling' of the yoni, in particular, a point just behind the clitoris. The Kamausadh can arouse even those women who are the most difficult to bring to sexual excitement.

Madankhush—the ring and middle fingers together create a mudra very aptly known as the Hook of Kamadeva, because it has the power to completely 'hook' the lover. When used to massage and scrape gently on the sides of the yoni, it is irresistible and will make the woman reach the heights of orgasm very quickly.

Manmathpataka or *Elephant Trunk*—the middle and little fingers are joined together to create this very versatile mudra that can be used in any direction to leave you feeling agitated and wanting more.

Stotra—the little finger is inserted on its own and churned round and round. The rest of the fingers balled up against the lips of the yoni create an additional circular massaging action that can prove hypnotic.

Pataka or *Flag*—this mudra represents the width and fluttery movement of a flag. Insert both the index and middle fingers into the yoni and then spread the fingers out and move them up and down in rapid motions. This will leave her clawing your back in her uncontainable arousal.

Trishul—the index and middle fingers are placed side by side, the ring finger is placed under them and they are inserted together and spread.

Shani Bhog—as above, but with all the fingers together side by side.

Karihast—this one also uses three fingers but here one joins the index and ring finger while keeping the middle finger separate and poised above the other two. Using all three fingers together has the advantage of taking several erogenous zones by surprise. It can create a combination of sensations that will take a woman from zero to sixty in record time. However, not all women can take the excitement of this mudra—some find it too agitating.

The study of ungli prayog, or the art of the fingers, was an intense and complex one because women are so diverse in their sexual needs and habits. Some women come to arousal very quickly and easily while others are extremely difficult to excite.

Each vulva is different in texture—smooth, rough, covered in knots and bumps, wrinkled in folds—the first being the most acutely responsive to any kind of touch, the next three progressively needing more and more stimulation. Different seasons, times of the month, phases of the moon also have an impact on sensitivity and arousal.

Fingers can do for a woman what nothing else can because they can access areas that are otherwise hard to penetrate. They can change the pressure, the touch and the sensations at will. There is no pleasure like it.

And it was an extremely useful tool for men as well. With the clever and judicious use of fingers a man could disguise his own weaknesses.

The *Kama Sutra* says that if the man's organ is inadequate he should use his fingers to bring his lover to full excitement and only after she has had her first orgasm should he penetrate her. This way she will be content at having reached her climax and be less likely to judge him for his lack of ability. His pride will remain intact.

If the man had the onus of satisfying several women (a harem), again the fingers were an excellent alternative. Far better than modern-day Viagra, using fingers is less exhausting, can provide more variety, put less pressure on the knees and back and has no side effects. Plus you could manage more than one woman at a time. Indian miniature paintings abound in depictions of kings pleasuring four different women at a time with the digits of each limb (fingers and toes of both hands and feet).

Another instance where fingers came in handy was if the yoni was too tight, leading to discomfort and no pleasure for either partner. The fingers could loosen and relax the area to prepare it for sex.

It was also common practice, in the case of kings and ministers, for the woman to be prepared beforehand (by maids or the harem eunuchs) for a night of lovemaking. Her yoni would be massaged and stimulated so that by the time she went to her lover she was in the right frame of mind.

If the fingers are used with dexterity and knowledge, the yoni will be like the proverbial water jar riddled with holes—very wet.

The ungli prayog of the *Kama Sutra* resonates with romance and seduction—it was about intensifying pleasure, not sexual gratification.

The mudras of ungli prayog were so evocative—of different pleasures, of different lovers, of different occasions—that they became part of the vocabulary of the epic romances of ancient and medieval India. Sanskrit and Tamil literatures of those periods were known for their exquisite descriptions, their ability to suggest the actions of lovers in delicious detail without ever baldly stating them. For instance, the mere mention of the Kamausadh mudra meant that the beloved was a woman who was used to many men and therefore needed a great deal of time and stimulation to come to arousal. There was no need for explicit langauge—it was enough to tell us that the lover had launched Kamausadh on his beloved for the reader to know that the 'swing of the God of love' (the vulva) would be conquered.

My Advice

The *Kama Sutra* says that a woman's heaven and hell reside between her legs—now is a good time to explore this, to understand how the fingers can be used for pleasure and fulfilment.

True seduction comes from within—it doesn't happen in emptiness. You have to fill yourself with the joy of your own sensuality, saturate your soul with it, allow it to radiate from you. You need to know what makes you happy before you can demand it from someone else.

Explore and be explored. Don't just leave it to your partner to pleasure you—become familiar with your own pleasure as well.

Ancient wisdom explains that the generating of pleasure is a shared act and yet pleasure spots are very individual—one cannot know what the other wants. Successful lovers teach each other what floats their boat.

Start with getting comfortable with your body. If you have never felt inside yourself perhaps today is the day to begin. The *Kama Sutra* says there are four distinct types of textures to the vulva—wouldn't you like to know yours? Also, if there are a few dozen erogenous spots in there, wouldn't it be interesting to see which ones work for you? If you can find what gives you enjoyment you can help your partner understand your needs better as well.

Set aside some time for yourself when you know you will not be interrupted. Keep enough time to enjoy the experience—this is 'you' time. Set the scene—a comfortable place with lots of room to move (you may find yourself rolling around from your stomach to your back). Choose the kind of lighting that works for you and apply some lubricant to your fingers—nothing heavy or sticky or messy, it'll only put you off. I suggest baby oil. And just have fun.

We must learn to take responsibility for ourselves. If you want your partner to be a good lover you have to first understand, at least to some extent, what makes your nerve endings go 'ping'—that way you can direct traffic more effectively.

There are dozens of combinations of fingers prescribed in the ancient love texts for ungli prayog but as with everything else, Vatsyayan reiterates that no matter how many lists he makes and how much information he gathers, there will always be something new or some variation that he hasn't thought of. Lovers are encouraged to try all sorts of new things, use all available knowledge to better themselves in the arts of seduction—but only after they experimented with everything that he has listed because there is no substitute for experience.

The great thing about using the fingers is that it's not difficult or exhausting and can bring equal pleasure to both partners.

Make it a bigger part of your seduction portfolio—not only does it offer you a place in heaven, the rewards right here are great too.

Dildos—Romance, Seduction, Fulfilment

Dildos were very important according to the *Kama Sutra*. Artificial devices and sexual aids were not about solitary masturbation—they were arts of seduction, tools that lovers could use to bring each other to greater heights of passion and fulfilment. In fact, metallurgy and woodwork are amongst the sixty-four essential skills mentioned in the *Kama Sutra*—so that lovers could make their own dildos.

The lover's main purpose during sex was to bring their partner to ultimate fulfilment through all the many arts of touching, loving and pleasuring taught by the *Kama Sutra*. But that was not always possible. For instance, if the genital sizes did not match—if the man was too small and the woman too large or vice versa—it could make things difficult. Or if there were multiple women to satisfy—as in a harem. Or if the man was impotent or weak, if he was too fat, if the woman had a very high sex drive, if it was a homosexual couple, if the woman wished to penetrate her partner, etc. There were many reasons why sexual fulfilment was not always possible.

In such cases, the *Kama Sutra* recommended using a device of some kind—because, as we've repeatedly seen, unsatisfactory sex was never an option. But, says Vatsyayan, if you are going to use a dildo it must be done properly—that is, by imitating the exact manner and thrusts of the superior lover so you can stimulate all the different erogenous points inside the yoni—because only then would the gates of heaven open and fulfilment be achieved.

The *Kama Sutra* recommends ten distinct strokes for using dildos.

Upasriptaka or *Straight In and Straight Out*—According to the *Kama Sutra* this is the best and 'most decent' way to have sex, where the dildo is moved in and out in the most straightforward fashion, 'like a wild horse bucking through a swiftly running stream'.[*] The perfect position is where the woman is lying down on her back with the legs raised and ankles supported. Vary the thrusts to suit your pleasure.

Manthana or *Churning*—The dildo is held in the hand and turned round and round as though you are churning the yoni 'like a flight of sea gulls wheeling around and playing in the waves'. It can be inserted to whatever depth you wish. As I've mentioned earlier, there are six erotic nerves that run through the length of the yoni, on all sides and at different depths—churning can excite all these points. It is said the pleasure from this can be so powerful that if the woman is not strong enough to handle it, she will faint.

Hula or *Rod* or *Piercing*—Here, the word 'piercing' means 'to plunge'. This dildo is used in a downward thrust but only to the tip of the vulva 'in the way that the sparrow picks out the grains of rice that have been left in the mortar'. Repeat

---

[*]Quotes on the styles of movement for dildos in this section are from *Sexual Secrets: The Alchemy of Ecstasy* by Nik Douglas and Penny Slinger, first published in 1979.

in constant and small movements. This is excellent for creating anticipation and building up excitement.

Avamardhana or *Devastator*—This is the same as the Hula, but here the dildo is plunged to the end of the vulva 'in the way that large stones sink when thrown into the sea'. For this movement the woman must lie on her back and arch her buttocks upwards in an almost ninety degree angle so as to allow unrestricted access. Placing a square pillow under the hips will help.

Piditaka or *Cruel*—This is once again the same as the Hula, but in this the dildo is removed some distance from the yoni and then brought down hard so that it penetrates the lips and drives through to the end with force, 'in the way that a frightened mouse rushes into its hole'. Once inside, continue to press hard for as long as it is bearable. Extra lubrication is essential to make sure that this is pleasurable rather than painful.

Nirghata or *Thunderbolt*—For this, the hips should be raised quite high with the help of a cushion. Maintain regular and gentle thrusts for a while and then stop for a long pause, thrust again for a while, stop again for a long pause, repeating till the vulva is lulled into a sleepy rhythm, and then suddenly let the dildo fall into the yoni again like an arrow 'rising and then plunging down, in the same way that the full sail of a boat braves a heavy gale'.

Varahaghata or *Thrust of the Wild Boar*—Lying on your side, face to face with your partner, rub the dildo with pressure in slow repetitions on only one side of the yoni, 'pushing in slowly, in the way that a snake enters its hole when about to hibernate for the winter'. Anyone who can pleasure his beloved in this manner will win her for all eternity. Even in the land of Yama she will not forget him.

Vrishaghata or *Thrust of the Bull*—This is like the Varahaghata, but here the dildo strikes two sides of the yoni in quick and alternate succession, 'flailing to the right and the left, in the same way a brave warrior breaks up the ranks of the enemy'.

Chitakavilasa or *Love Game of the Bird*—Alternate between deep and shallow thrusts, changing the rhythm constantly, like the pecking of a bird. It is a great way to bring the lovemaking to climax.

Samputa or *Box*—Lying down absolutely straight, on top of each other, insert the dildo. Do not thrust, just press in small movements as you lie together, just as a hawk skims the ground with his feet when trying to grab an elusive rabbit. The Samputa does not depend so much on the position; it is more about the movement of the device. The pressing is supposed to be the most pleasurable sensation of all and a favourite with most people.

Sexual devices and aids came in all sizes and shapes—small ones, big ones, huge ones of almost intimidating proportions, ones that looked like gymnastic equipment and even some that would have taken a small army to operate. But the most popular device seems to have been the humble dildo. In spite of its lack of glamour and artistic creativity it was obviously the most practical, the safest and—so long as you could learn how to thrust and move it properly—most likely to deliver results.

Lovers were encouraged to make their own dildos. As I've mentioned, according to the *Kama Sutra*, vulvas are different not only in size and sensitivity, but also in stimulation levels. Some are smooth and soft and need very little stimulation to come to arousal, some are rough and covered with knots and bumps and require far more friction to get them going; what was exciting for one could be painful for another, what was pleasantly rough here was boringly smooth there. A one-size-fits-all dildo would not really do the job—it was best to make one for yourself to perfectly suit your own needs.

Therefore, metallurgy and woodwork was one of the sixty-four essential skills for lovers mentioned in the *Kama Sutra* so that dildos could be made customized for specific arousal types.

Dildos could be made of precious metals like gold or silver, ordinary metals like tin or lead or even different types of wood. The best kinds were the wooden ones because, once polished and thoroughly oiled, they had the most natural feel of all. When covered with well-oiled leather, this made it as close to the real thing as possible.

If one had to use a metal one, then tin was the best because, when inserted, this felt cool and soft like semen and had a 'pleasant roughness'. But if the dildo was going to be a gift from a lover, then the *Kama Sutra* said that no woman worth her salt should accept anything other than one made of gold— she is to say 'this is the one that feels most like you when it is inside me. It makes me think of you and my love is increased.'

In a pinch, if nothing else was available, the *Kama Sutra* says that fruits and vegetables of the right shape work equally well, like bamboo, gourds, cucumber. They should be rigorously cleaned and rubbed with either oil or honey before use. In the end, the most natural product is the best.

Sometimes the dildo was made to be worn as a sheath. It was a hollow contraption that opened and closed like a suit of armour to wear over the penis in order to have sex in the 'normal' way—in case of impotence or weak erections. In ancient India, something as trifling as impotence was never an obstacle to sex. The sheath dildo was made with protective guards at the base to cover the testicles to prevent it from slipping backwards during a moment of excitement and slicing something off. This little prosthetic could be made of wood or metal. It was generally covered with leather and then attached to the waist with elastic bands to make it as close to the real thing as possible. And it came highly recommended for its psychological benefits—knowing that you were physically penetrating your lover was excellent for the ego.

Dildos were almost always strapped to the waist so that the lover had his hands free to pleasure his partner in other ways as well. They would be held in place with the help of bands and twine, sometimes as many as three or four straps. Dildos could occasionally be decorated with beads and other things to add texture, size and beauty.

But whatever the shape or style, the ultimate goal was fulfilment and pleasure. And for this reason the masters taught the art of moving and thrusting the dildo.

My Advice

Let's change our attitudes towards the dildo. Forget about using one for a masturbation routine—try using one to romance your partner.

Pay special attention to the movements and strokes, learn the styles and thrusts—let it be a gift to the beloved.

Have you ever considered using a dildo with your partner? Or thought about how you could use one to try out some of the more acrobatic portions of the *Kama Sutra*?

Several of the movements that the *Kama Sutra* talks about above are either extremely difficult or entirely impossible for most people, but we know that they would be extraordinarily pleasurable. For instance, the Churning has been voted the top stroke for female pleasure, but quite honestly if you were to follow the sexual routine of the actual position, it would require an upper body strength that is beyond most of us.

The answer lies in the dildo.

Lubrication is very necessary.

Interestingly, the Chinese erotic texts discourage using anything oily or sugary to lubricate the vulva, as it could cause an infection. Saliva or glycerine water, very similar to KY jelly, was considered better.

The Indian texts however regularly recommend the use of oil and honey. The best thing is to be sensible and cautious about it. Do your homework on your options and pick the lubricant that is right for you.

Kissing

'Forgive the shortcomings of this wretch...since the kisses I practice during the night are forbidden to me during the day.'[*]

There are sixty-four categories of kisses listed in the *Kama Sutra*, but Vatsyayan says that there are hundreds of variations and permutations of kissing according to local customs and personal preferences. For instance, there is mention of communities that like to kiss the underarm hair of their lovers. There are kisses for first time lovers, secret ways of kissing your lover in public and even a very specific kiss if you wanted an expensive gift.

In some regions, people were only allowed to kiss between ten at night and three in the morning—kissing in the daytime was strictly forbidden.

We don't operate under any of these restrictions any more—you can kiss anytime and anywhere—and yet where is the satisfaction? So few people still really get it right!

The act of kissing involves 34 facial muscles and 112 postural muscles, and kissing on the mouth is the closest you will get

---

[*]Alain Daniélou, *The Complete Kama Sutra,* New York: Simon and Schuster, 1993. (King Nala, noticing that his beloved new bride, Damayanti, was looking unsatisfied, sends her this message through her maid.)

to the act of sex before the actual act (the mouth most closely resembles the sexual organs—the tongue is like the penis, the lips and cavity of the mouth resemble the yoni and its lips). A kiss can be the most erotically stimulating thing and yet at the same time utterly romantic—it can stimulate your erotic nerve centres, it can bring you to orgasm, it can addle your brain, it can reduce you to a quivering heap of inarticulate jelly.

And yet, it is something we are happy to muddle through—sloppy tongues, dribbling mouths, wrong place, wrong time—all in the name of the kiss.

You could spend a lifetime experimenting with different types of kisses. I am only going to look at a few of these, but I hope you will practice all sorts of variants on your own and find out all the hidden secrets of the kiss for yourself.

According to the *Kama Sutra*, kissing is the most important part of the love game. Foreplay should begin with kissing and it should continue to accompany everything else during sex. Lips, says Vatsyayan, hold an electric charge, and when you place your lips on your lover's lips—or on any other part of their body—the charge is transferred to the nerves, and excitement arises everywhere.

The *Kama Sutra* says that people who are very sexually excitable don't need any rules to guide them, but those who are not quite so 'active' need help as they can end up feeling quite confused about how to proceed. This is not a judgement on your sexual prowess. What this really means is that as you get further and further into lovemaking, and passion grows, rules become unnecessary. But it is a mistake to think that in the beginning there is no need for any. In the throes of passion, lovers suck on each other 'like sugar lumps', it does not matter what part of the body you kiss and how—a cake is sweet no matter where you bite into it. But to approach that state of mindless ecstasy, a great deal of mindfulness is necessary. The 'seed of desire, born of mutual attraction must develop' and that needs delicacy and knowledge—it has to be watered with the 'ambrosia' of the right kind of kisses and caresses. If you want to get to that point of passion, if you want your lover melting in your arms and wanting to tear your clothes off, then it is really important to understand what will take you there and, as you will see with this chapter, often it is just a few simple techniques.

The first kiss, that first touch of lovers, is very important. Did you know elephants can come to full orgasm at the first touch—think how much more important this is for humans. That first kiss can make or break your chances as a lover. Vatsyayan says that for the first kiss, don't begin by sticking your tongue down your partner's throat—no grabbing, no pulling, no groping. Not only will it not give them any pleasure, it may put them off sex with you for good.

The first kiss is not literally always the very first kiss that you will exchange. It could also be the first kiss of the day, it could be the first kiss after some time apart, it could be a kiss at any time that one wishes. We call it the first kiss because it is charmingly tentative and utterly delicate—like new love. What we are referring to as the first kiss is in fact a combination of what the *Kama Sutra* catalogues as the first three kisses—*Nimittaka* or *Nominal Kiss*, *Sphuritaka* or *Vibrant Kiss* and *Ghattitaka* or *Rubbing Kiss*. But actually these should be treated as the three steps of one kiss. According to the *Kama Sutra*, the aim of the man with this first kiss is to make gentle contact with the lips, making the kiss so irresistible that it gradually convinces your partner to prolong it.

Keeping your eyes open and talking softly, lean in and place your lower lip on your partner's lower lip with a feather touch. It is what the *Kama Sutra* refers to as the Nimittaka (or

Nominal Kiss). It should be the barest of touches. Now very, very gently rub her lip with yours, with absolutely no force, only enough to make her lip quiver slightly. If this is the very first time you are kissing do not use hands at all. If you have kissed before, then begin by holding her head in place with your hands or curving a strand of her hair around your finger and holding her head in place with the help of that. For the next step (Sphuritaka), give little delicate kisses to her closed mouth like a woodpecker, alternating between the upper and lower lip. Occasionally pause to spend a bit more time at the opening of her lips, but do not force them open.

The third part of the kiss (Ghattitaka), according to the *Kama Sutra*, is the response that comes from the partner (but there are no hard and fast rules—either partner can carry on the kiss). However, if you have done it right, by now you should have her quivering with anticipation and, desperate with unfulfilled desire, she will close her eyes and try and hold your lip in hers to stop you from moving away.

The *Kama Sutra* says that the woman will feel acutely shy at the thought of her own arousal and so she places one hand over her lover's eyes and the other over her own and, taking his lower lip in her teeth, she will try to bite it or run her tongue over it. She is so aroused she can no longer contain herself, but is so embarrassed by her lustful thoughts that she covers both their eyes—now the world cannot be witness to her shamelessness. The first flush of passion is better felt than seen. So it is time to shut the eyes and the kiss can be deepened into a bite or you can use the tongue to rub against her lip—but that is as far as you should go. Use all your willpower to restrain yourself even if you or your lover need more. Build it up like you have never done before. The rewards will be fantastic.

There are several variations to this kiss. You can seize

both the lips of your lover in your mouth and suck on them with tongue, teeth and lips—but the book says this is only enjoyable with hairless lips. If the man has a moustache it could be disagreeable. You can cup your lover's lips in your fingers and kiss them while rubbing them with your thumb. You can massage the lower gums or the inside of the lower lip with your tongue. But remember—the essence of this kiss is that the tongue must never go beyond the teeth.

No rushing, no drool, no fumbling or groping—the only touch should be a very quick one on the hair or the chin.

Even if the relationship is a long-standing one, it is still worth playing with this kiss—it adds romance, creates anticipation and freshens up desire.

Raga Dipana or *Inflamer Kiss* is a simple yet very effective kiss of seduction. When your lover is asleep, wake him up with kisses and embraces—he will know how much you want him and that will make him melt. This kiss is given when you want to reignite passion as well as when you want an expensive gift.

Instead of having sex and then going to sleep as one normally does, do it the other way round—go to sleep and then have sex. Not only is there an element of newness to this, but also the changing positions of the moon as the night progresses mean that your sexual inclinations change too, and you make love differently.

Just as different ragas (musical compositions) are played according to the time of day, so too sexual desires, intensities and acts change according to the time of the night. The position known as the Mare's Trick is best performed after the Inflamer Kiss. ('When, like a mare, Cruelly gripping a stallion, Your lover traps and milks your penis, With her vagina, It is Vadavaka or the Mare's Trick'.[*])

---

[*]From *The Kama Sutra of Vatsyayan* translated by Sir Richard Burton, 1883.

The Inflamer Kiss is best given about one or two hours before dawn because at this time the body needs far less time to come to arousal. Bending over your lover, allowing your hair to brush over his face and chest, hold his lips with your fingers and kiss and bite his lower lip insistently—inflame him.

A similar kiss, but done by the man, is the *Pratibodhika* or *Awakening*. This is when the lover returns home late at night and kisses his sleeping beloved in order to wake her up and make love. But this kiss can have many a pitfall. If the girl wants to test his feelings she will pretend to be asleep. If he does not kiss her on his arrival she will assume that he has had his fill somewhere else and this can lead to a fight.

The *Kama Sutra* lists four special kisses that use the tongue, the teeth and the lips together, and are expressly not given on the mouth.

Sama or *Flat Kiss*—this kiss is especially for the sensitive flesh on the inside of the joints—the back of the knee, the crook of the elbow, the very ticklish spot where the thighs meet the hip etc. Sitting or lying down next to each other, these areas should be nibbled gently and probed and tickled with the tongue. The kiss should be neither too soft nor too hard. Just as a good chef will prepare the dish in a way that you can taste the individual flavours of each ingredient, so it should be with these sensitive spots. To get the real flavour of this kiss you should be able to feel each incursion separately.

Pidita or *Pressed Kiss*—this is a far more vigorous kiss given on the raised mounds of flesh—cheeks, breasts, buttocks, hips etc. Pressing, kneading and agitating the flesh, energetically use the lips and tongue to massage while sinking your teeth into those parts of the body. Remember, however, there must be no pain and definitely no marks left.

Ashchita or *Curling Kiss*—this kiss is for the hidden wells of delight—the parts of the body that are sunken in and hidden, like a cave. These areas are the luscious fragrant flesh that hides under the full breast, the swirling eddy of the navel, the heavenly dip of the yoni. Using the tongue explore and reveal these areas, using the teeth scrape ever so lightly as to cause goose bumps—but nothing more. This kiss should be used to stir up desire and create cravings but it should offer no relief or fulfilment. This kiss should be your secret weapon, something that makes your lover desperate for you.

Mridu or *Delicate Kiss*—after you have raked up a frenzy of desire and driven her mad with passion, it is time to soothe the itch. Using the lips, tongue and teeth, calm the back, hips, buttocks and breasts, bring her storm to tranquillity.

The thought of sexual intimacy in public places, with the imminent fear of being found out at any time, is obviously not a modern-day invention, it seems to have been a fantasy since the beginning of time. There were various ways to kiss your lover in public without being seen. You could blow a very discreet kiss with your fingers pointing to the feet of the beloved, you could enthusiastically kiss a small child who happened to be on the scene while looking at the lover, you could kiss the shadow of the beloved on the wall or the reflection in water. The *Kama Sutra* even offers a secret-public kiss where you could physically connect with the beloved—it was called the Kiss and Drop. Imagine the scene—a public fete, hundreds of people milling around, you walked up close to your lover and then, pretending to be overcome with heat, suddenly dropped to the floor as though in a faint—but as you fell you would plant a kiss on your lover's thigh or big toe.

Bending the Head Kiss—'Bending your head' to kiss meant that you were going to kiss the genitals. For this kiss the shape of the tongue is most important. If it is for cunnilingus, penetrate with the tongue and open it out as flat and broad as you can—this gives the most pleasure. If it is for fellatio, use different formations of the tongue—long with the tip rolled into a point, flat and open, flat and vibrating. This one is a hidden kiss, men who indulge in it do not talk about it to their peers. In the time of the *Kama Sutra* social norms seem to have had an ambiguous relationship with oral sex. It was both popularly practised and strenuously shunned. Men of upper castes did not perform oral sex, and if they thought that the woman might have done so with someone else, they did not kiss her on the mouth either. But at the same time the woman's mouth was considered pure during sex, so oral sex would not have contaminated her. The *Kama Sutra* argues with itself about the pleasures and evils of this kiss but finally settles on the condition that it can be practised with a courtesan but not with the wife.

The Spoken and Unspoken Kiss—The 'Spoken' or Sa-shabd kiss is simply one which is accompanied by sighs or moans. A great deal of emphasis was laid on the sounds of sex which were meant to enhance the experience. The 'Unspoken' or Ni-shabd kiss is where no sounds are made. The 'spoken' kiss was considered better—it was far more arousing.

When using the tongue to penetrate or probe different parts of the body (mouth, yoni, navel, armpit etc.), changing the shape of the tongue will alter the movement of the tongue and that in turn will change the sensations. The three most popular shapes are penetrating with the flat tongue for a soft exploration; rolling the tongue and penetrating with a sharp tip for a harder massage; and entering with the flat tongue and then vibrating it in a trembling motion. The last is said to be the most exciting of all but the book says it needs a lot of practice.

My Advice

The study of kissing is known as philematology. Yes, there is an entire branch of academia that focuses on kissing; you need never feel that you are putting too much time into studying the perfect way to kiss—others have spent more.

Although the kiss is a natural human instinct and has existed from the beginning of time—crabs and spiders have been observed in the act—anthropologist Vaughn Bryant's research shows that the kiss as we know it may have originated from India and been spread westwards by Alexander the Great.

We know from the *Kama Sutra* that kissing was considered the most important of all sexual acts and has been described in enormous detail. In ancient India, it was believed that kissing had magical powers. Through the exchange of saliva one could pull out the soul, put someone under a spell or breathe new life into a person.

And yet India has lost the art of kissing. Writer Indra Sinha points out that between the thirteenth century CE, when artists sculpted the walls of the Konark temple with passionately embracing couples, and the 1978 Bollywood film *Satyam Shivam Sundaram*, kissing disappeared from Indian public life.

Everyone should practise and perfect the 'First Kiss'. Anyone can go harder but going soft till you have your partner clawing and trembling with passion, begging you to go harder—now that's a skill! Do your homework—it will bring unimaginable dividends.

Now think—how often do you kiss your partner? I mean

really kiss them, as in a full-on, mouth glued to mouth, all-the-time-in-the-world type of kiss. Not often? Even less? Just when you have sex? So I need you to try what sexologists call the ten-second kiss. Once a day—you decide whether it will be first thing in the morning or in the evening after work or whatever works for you—but *every* single day. Put your arms around your partner and really smooch him or her for ten whole seconds. Count in your head if necessary. Ten seconds is a very long time, as you will realize—most kisses (or what we think of as intense kisses) are about three seconds long unless you are about to have sex. Ten seconds is long enough to make a connection—it will get your partner's full attention. It is long enough to create an impression—it will stick in their mind: when they think of the kiss, they think of you. And most importantly a kiss is the language of love and pleasure—it will leave your partner feeling cherished and create a bond.

Kissing has many a health benefit. It can cure headaches and relieve blood pressure, it can fight cavities and create temporary facelifts, it can make the skin glow and burn calories. And of course it is the perfect barometer for good sex—good kiss = good sex.

Oral Sex

In 342 CE, the ecumenical council of the Catholic Church passed a law banning oral and anal sex. Sex was a necessary evil, you had it only in order to reproduce. There was nothing remotely utilitarian about oral sex—it was purely for pleasure—and therefore it was bad for the soul.

Coincidentally, across the oceans, Vatysayayan too was shaking his head over oral sex—he had decided it could be bad for health.

The problem was, he said, that people always tended to have oral sex in the same way, they focus on the same spot and end up stimulating the same nerves each time. This could lead to some nerves becoming over stimulated and eventually desensitized, and some other nerves not getting any stimulation at all—leading to long-term sensory imbalance, constrictions in the blood vessels and, potentially, even impotence.

The genitals are packed with nerve endings which connect to all the different organs. Each time you kiss one part it impacts the corresponding organ and if just one part (of the penis or the yoni) is stimulated over and over again while the rest are ignored, it can create an imbalance in that organ. For instance, the clitoris is connected to the kidneys, and as you go deeper inside the yoni you have the nerve endings for the heart, lungs, etc. If just the clitoris gets stimulated each time, eventually it will cause kidney-related issues like bladder control problems, memory loss, back and knee pain, while other organs like the heart and the lungs will be under-stimulated and develop their own problems. In a man, the tip of the penis is connected to the lungs and overstimulation of the tip can lead to lung-related problems.

Vatsyayan says if people wanted to have oral sex it was essential they learn exactly how it should be done so that it can be both pleasurable and beneficial—at what points of the genitals the kisses should be placed, what the tongue movements should be, how long should each one last, in what sequence, and so on.

The *Kama Sutra* offers a careful education for both fellatio and cunnilingus.

There are eight specific methods of fellatio:

Begin with *Nimitta* or *Casual Touch*—holding the penis in one hand, place your lips gently around the tip and move your head in small semicircles. It should be like a half kiss, using the inside of the lips.

Parshavatodashta or *Nibbling the Sides*—holding the penis from the top, nibble alternately with the lips and the teeth, very gently on one side, all the way up and down, then on the other side in the same way.

Bahiha-Samdansha or *External Pinching*—After the penis has been stimulated by nibbling, it is time to increase the pressure. You can now alternate between kissing and sucking the tip of the penis.

Antaha-Samdansha or *Internal Pinching*—This is when the shaft is taken deep into the mouth and sucked hard. The man is ready to come and wants more friction. The *Kama Sutra* says this kiss will inflame the man so much that at this point, he will pay extra to increase the tempo.

Chumbitaka or *Kiss*—Instead of increasing the tempo, the woman will use this kiss to slow things down. It is still too early for him to come, so the penis is removed from the mouth and held in the hand and the lips are used to dot little kisses on the top.

Parimrshtaka or *Striking at the Tip*—Still holding the penis in the hand it is time to lash at it repeatedly with the tongue. The tip of the tongue is rolled into a sharp point and used like a whip.

Amrachushita or *Sucking the Mango*—Taking half the penis into the mouth, suck on it hard—like you would the flesh of a mango from its seed.

Sangara or *Devoured Whole*—When he is close to orgasm, take the whole penis in your mouth and using the pressure of the tongue and lips, make him come.

It is not necessary to swallow the semen. Some people will lick off the small amounts that appear at the tip, some are happy to swallow it all while others will spit it all out. That is a matter of choice.

Those are the eight ways to fellate.

Equally there are eight ways to perform cunnilingus.

Before you begin with cunnilingus, the first thing to understand is the benefits of the different shapes of the tongue when pleasuring a woman.

If you change the shape of the tongue, this will alter its movement and that in turn will change the sensations. The three most popular shapes are:

Soochi—penetrate with the flat tongue for a soft exploration.

Pratati—roll the tongue and penetrate with a sharp tip for a harder massage.

Vaakali—enter with the flat tongue and then vibrate it in a trembling motion. This is said to be the most exciting of all, but it needs a lot of practice.

The function of the first kiss it to get the yoni accustomed to your touch and to the sensations that are about to follow. Begin by delicately closing the lips of the yoni and holding them together, kiss the area, rubbing and agitating it with your lips. This is known as the *Quivering Kiss*.

This is followed by the *Circling Tongue* in which, using your forefinger and thumb, you spread open the lips of the yoni and probe the entrance with your nose and tongue. But you should stay at the entrance—it is not yet time to enter further.

The Tongue Massage is where you enter deeper and massage vigorously with the tongue. This will get the juices flowing and thoroughly lubricate the inside.

Next it is time for the *Chushita* or *The Sucked*. Use the teeth, the tongue and the lips together to nibble just on the inside of the opening of the yoni while sucking on the clitoris.

As the excitement mounts, kiss her with the *Uchchushita* or *The Sucked Up*. Raise her buttocks with either a crescent shaped cushion or by placing your hands under her. Now run your tongue from her navel down her abdomen into the entrance of her vulva. This will awaken the erotic nerves in the navel and set the juices flowing more copiously.

Massaging the tops of the thighs and playing with them, pulling them together and then apart again, enter her with your tongue in the *Kshobhaka* or *Stirring*.

As she lies on her back, kneel in front of her and, placing her knees on your shoulders, bend down and kiss her while playing with the curve of her waist. This is known as the *Bahuchushita*.

And, finally, the position that has come to be known as '69' and what the *Kama Sutra* calls the *Kakila*. Lie face to feet and enjoy each other with your tongues and lips.

Such is the pleasure of oral sex that women have been known to abandon the company of good and decent patrons who are also wealthy and generous for a lover of unsteady character and no money just because he will indulge them with cunnilingus.

The *Kama Sutra* has a strange and contradictory relationship with oral sex.

It begins by saying that it does not recommend oral sex and that decent people should not indulge in it, while simultaneously telling us that it is the most pleasurable of all sexual acts and then going into great detail about how it should be done in order to maximize that pleasure.

It is constantly swinging between telling us 'it is against societal norms, don't do it' and 'it is very pleasurable, this is how you do it'. It is not permitted, but still permitted, it is not pure but still pure, it is not healthy but still healthy!

According to the law books of dharma the mouth is pure, it should only be used for eating or saying prayers, not sullied by touching the genitals. But the same dharma says that during sex, the woman's mouth is pure and cannot be sullied no matter what act she performs.

However, kings and ministers are urged to set an example and not perform oral sex. If they find themselves with a woman who is known to have done it with someone else, they should not even consent to kiss her on the mouth, as even that could pollute them.

Often eunuchs and transvestites (hijras) were employed to fellate the men of higher classes since there was less expectation of reciprocation. Unlike with a courtesan, you did not have to 'return the favour'—at most you would pinch their nipples as a mutual expression of arousal—but there was absolutely no need for kissing (no exchange of saliva meant no danger of polluting the mouth with leftover semen or other fluids). One did not did judge the eunuchs and transvestites for performing oral sex as this was their only way of earning a living.

The law books continue—it was okay to have oral sex for one's personal pleasure but only with someone you paid; under no circumstances could you ask your wife to do this for you because that was a sin so heinous that it would affect not just your future generations but even your dead ancestors (the ancestors or pitiris would lose fifteen years of their heavenly merits and their nirvana would be set back by one lifetime). However, in some regions of India, oral sex is an acceptable practice and if the wife comes from one of these places then she should be allowed to perform it without any kind of judgement or censure. And in this case it is not a sin.

There was also the question of the sexual fluids themselves. They were believed to be more potent than the most powerful tonics and the health benefits of ingesting them were considerable. Semen is made up of 60 per cent vitamins and

40 per cent essential minerals—it is the most natural energy booster. In Ancient China, emperors would have their servants collect the semen of healthy young men, which was then mixed with herbs and taken as medicine. In Tantra, there is a position called the Vajroli Mudra in which the man, instead of ejaculating his semen, can be taught to reverse the flow so that not only does his semen get reabsorbed into his own body, but he can suck up the woman's fluids as well.

The *Kama Sutra* does not mention anything about ingesting semen but all the other sexual and medical texts of the East treat it as a very important subject, including the Chinese texts (such as *Secret Methods of the Plain Girl, Arts of the Bedchamber*, etc.), Ayurvedic and Tantric works. It does, however, tell us that the taste and smell of sexual fluids, which is the most common hesitation people have when it comes to oral sex, depends on what you eat and how much you drink—particularly alcohol. Vatsyayan says that the less alcohol you drink the better your sexual fluids taste.

It is difficult to know whether the *Kama Sutra* approves of oral sex or not—as I've said, it tells us in equal measure not to do it but also how to do it. But whether it approves of it or not it clearly acknowledges this to be an extraordinarily pleasurable act to which maximum attention should be paid.

The tongue is the second most powerful muscle in the body, it is warm, it is wet and it is mobile and when accompanied by the lips and the teeth, it can create explosive sensations.

My Advice

Oral sex is the most intimate act you will ever perform with your partner, even more than penetrative sex. The combination of the power of the tongue, the sensitivity of the lips and friction of the teeth can provide more sensations than anything else. We talk about the immense power, the ultimate pleasure and variety—not till you have experienced the mouth down there will you understand the true meaning of this. Add to that the fact that you can use your hands over other parts of the body at the same time—an immeasurable advantage.

But aside from the physical excitement this is one act where the mind also gets involved consciously. It is a combination of passion and stillness. There is a feeling of being completely in the moment.

In regular sex, pleasure depends on the penis being able to access certain erotic nerves and to access them with the right amount of pressure—some nerves need less pressure than others and, depending on the time of month and the season, different nerves need stimulating in different ways. The size and placement of the genitals mean that the positions and movements needed to fit them together are not always organic.

All this is not a problem in oral sex. Because there is such intense pleasure and because there is no insecurity on the continuation of that pleasure—that if you lose the rhythm the friction will decrease—there is no frenzy or panic to 'get it right'. Both mind and body slow down and create a stillness that in turn allows you to feel all the subtle little sensations that you did not even know existed. It is your chance to explore pleasure at your own pace.

Get comfortable with each other's genitals. Science tells us that the pheromones produced during excitement make the groin area of both men and women smell wonderful—enjoy the smell.

Hygiene is paramount; the entire area should be really clean—any hint of smell or sweat will put your partner off for life. The men of the *Kama Sutra* were expected to shave their pubic regions regularly to keep the area free of sweat and smell. It was a very strictly laid down regime—pubic hair was shaved every five days and waxed every ten days. The area was also kept free of sweat by wiping with a special cloth and perfuming. This was the mark of the sophisticated man.

Diet decides what our sexual fluids taste like—we are what we eat and we taste of it. Semen doesn't actually taste of anything at all but can take on an unpleasant flavour owing to an illness or excessive alcohol intake, etc. Alcohol is one of the biggest factors—laying off alcohol and drinking a lot more water, even for one week, can completely transform the taste of you.

Don't stress about swallowing. Oral sex doesn't have to end with orgasm. Going down on someone is best done in short spurts. If, as a woman, you are unsure about swallowing, try licking off little bits from the tip of the penis. The tip is constantly being moistened with tiny bits of ejaculate—pick it up with the finger and taste it, see how you feel about it. Or don't ingest at all—perform oral sex for a while and then finish with penetrative sex. As a man, you can coat your partner's yoni with a flavoured lubricant like chocolate or honey or whatever else works for you—you get lubricants in all kinds of flavours these days. It may be useful to disguise the sexual fluids till you have a chance to get used to them.

Work on the whole organ and use every bit of the tongue and your lips for mutual pleasure.

And, finally, don't overdose on oral sex. Not just the *Kama Sutra*, even the Chinese texts say one should not have oral sex too often as the excess of sensations (although wonderful) can lead to a gradual loss of feeling in the area.

Everything in moderation is a good motto for almost anything in life.

Feet

Legend has it that when the entertainment for the heavens was being decided Indra had specifically asked for dance. He could visualize those beautiful feet moving like lightning, twisting and turning into inconceivable mudras, able to stamp out rhythms that even the musicians struggled with. What magic there was in a foot! Place it this way and one little ghungroo would quiver tentatively to life, place it that way and it could send the universe pounding. What sensitivity, what discipline, what love was that foot capable of! The refined foot was worthy of worship.

The Apsaras (celestial dancers of Indra's court) are the patron deities of seduction, the mistresses of the refined foot, and dance is the very first of the sixty-four essential skills of the *Kama Sutra*.

There is a whole language of feet in the love traditions of Sanskrit poetry—it has been carved into the Ajanta sculptures, it has been etched into the verses of the *Rasatarangini*, it has been immortalized in the dance of the Apsaras and, according to some scholars, it may even have been the original inspiration behind the Chinese foot fetish. Howard Levy, author of *Chinese*

96

Footbinding: The History of a Curious Erotic Custom, says that the Chinese obsession with feet was born out of Indian dance traditions while other scholars feel that ancient India's romance with the foot came from China, via the courtesans.

It was the courtesans' job to learn all the newest trends in sex—the more she knew the more desirable she was and the higher her status. Since it was customary for all men of high position, when entering a city, to first pay their respects to these courtesans, they were required to have vast knowledge—they could be called upon to do anything to entertain the visitors. And with the number of visitors coming from China, it would have only made sense for courtesans of the time to be familiar with, if not masters of, Chinese foot erotica.

In reality, it could easily have been either. Two thousand years ago there seems to have been a surprising amount of travel between countries and cultures; literature and traditions were carried back and forth and absorbed, creating some new, and some shared, practices. Ancient Indian and Chinese texts share a great deal of knowledge and wisdom on all subjects ranging from sexual practices to medicine to horticulture to Vastu (Feng Shui)—even foot erotica.

The Chinese believed that the foot (which they called the 'golden lotus flower') was the most intimate part of the woman's body and just to hold it was tantamount to having sex. The ancient Chinese had more variations of holding the foot in the hand than the number of sexual positions in the *Kama Sutra*—how to lift the foot, with what pressure to grasp it, when to encase it with the fingers, when to move it to the palms, two hands, one hand—it was the source of hours of pleasure and repeated orgasms. Levy writes, 'Play included kissing, sucking and inserting the foot in the mouth until it filled both cheeks, either nibbling at it or chewing vigorously, and adoringly placing it against one's cheeks, chest, knees or virile member.' One of the most highly sought after practices of foreplay was to eat almonds from between the toes of the lover. Men would pay in gold to watch a woman manipulating almonds between her toes. And then to be fed those same almonds was to know new heights of ecstasy.

The ancient Chinese practice of foot binding was not only aimed at making the feet tiny but also to reshape them to serve different purposes. The big toe, for instance, was left to grow abnormally large (or perhaps it just looked that big compared to the rest of the foot), to resemble a small penis or an extra-large clitoris. The arch was so deeply pronounced that when the woman put both feet together the arches created a sort of cavity, much like the vulva.

However, there is a world of difference between Chinese fetish and the *Kama Sutra*'s refined and delicate romance with the feet. Like the Chinese 'golden lotus flower' the Sanskrit term for the foot is also 'charan kamal' or 'lotus feet', but that is as far as the similarities go. The Chinese foot fixation was coloured by the language of dominance and control—'binding', 'tying', 'immobilizing', etc. whereas for the ancient Indians, the highly trained foot was exciting for its mobility, not its captivity.

Indian dance costumes were especially made to show the feet—the ankles elongated with ghungroos, the arches highlighted with alta to beautify the feet. And then to watch them move—quick as lightning or slow as dripping honey, each movement calculated to set the senses on fire.

In poetic metaphor the mention of the lover worshiping at the beloved's 'charan kamal' meant that he had placed her lotus feet to his head, i.e. made love. If the lover wanted to discreetly acknowledge his beloved in public, he would pick up a lotus flower and touch it to his head.

There is a footnote to the public (but secret) kiss I mentioned earlier, wherein if you had the urge to kiss the beloved, you would walk up to her and pretend to fall—suddenly drop at her feet and place a quick, discreet kiss on her foot. If help did not arrive immediately the *Kama Sutra* says you would take the opportunity to briefly suck on her toe.

One of the major erotic nerve endings (see chapter Erotic Nerves) is located in the big toe of the left foot and can be stimulated at different points of the foot—in the toe, under the arch, at the pad of the foot, on top of the foot, at the ankle, etc.

In the cycle of shifting erogenous zones the foot falls on the very first day, the new moon, so it was important to get it right. It was the first portal for the erotic energies to start flowing. If this was not done right the rest of the cycle would have blockages.

The foot could be stimulated by rubbing, pressing, striking or pinching. The woman whose vulva is cool and smooth on the inside and outside, like the petals of a lotus flower, should have her feet rubbed to stimulate her. The woman whose vulva is round and soft and quick to become wet on the inside and not too hairy on the outside—her foot should be pressed. She who is long, deep set and very hairy should have her foot struck with the open palm. The woman whose vulva is very wide inside and covered with soft down on the outside needs to have her foot pinched to be fully aroused.

Since every woman's erotic threshold is different, the pressure applied to the feet for arousal also varied. The woman whose joints are not prominent needs just a gentle touch, the woman whose joints are very prominent needs to have her feet excited with love bites, the woman whose upper joints are prominent but the lower ones are not—her feet need to be stimulated with love scratches and the woman who has prominent lower joints only, her feet need the hardest pressure of all.

Arousal, especially in a woman, did not flare up all at once, it came gradually, in stages. When playing with the foot, it was suggested to start with the ankle, move to the top of the foot, then the arch under the foot, then the pad of the foot, before ending with the big toe.

Ideally, one should be lying down or leaning against something when working on the foot. If you wish to accompany it with sex then the *Kama Sutra* recommends specific positions. You can be in the traditional position—the woman down with her ankles on the man's shoulders as he kneels in front of her. As you make love you can take the beloved's foot in your mouth. The other option is the 'Crow' position (also known as the 69). The woman should take her place on top, but instead of lying full length, she should tuck her knees under her, near the man's chest, so that it is her feet that reach his face.

My Advice

There is an entire genre of ancient erotic literature (in Sanskrit, Tamil and other Indian languages) based on the metaphor of the lover placing his head under the feet of the beloved.

The foot is very sexy. Every culture across the world has had some kind of erotica attached to the foot. And it is versatile. You can use it to flirt, you can use it to seduce, you can even use it to have sex.

It is said that a woman who has never experienced a 'foot job' does not know true orgasm.

Ancient erotic texts said it was because the foot was just so full of nerve endings that it couldn't help but be excitable. Modern science says it is because in the brain the 'foot nerves' sit right next to the 'erotic impulse nerves' and that the erotic stimulation spills over. The ancient love texts recommend more ornamentation for the foot than any other part of the body.

The underside of the foot can be painted with alta, or even henna, to highlight the arches and make the colour of the skin appear more striking. Anklets and toe rings attached to each other with delicate chains elongate the foot and make it look slimmer. Nails should be well shaped and painted. The foot can be perfumed with a floral or citrus scent.

Keep your feet mobile—mobility is provocative. When you want to flirt, kick off your sandals, display the arch and flex your foot, let it be theatre.

Play footsie. And do a lot more.

The Art of Thrusting

Whenever we think of adding an element of surprise or excitement to our sex lives, when we think we want to introduce something new to break the monotony, we automatically either turn to new positions or new geography—let's try the sofa, let's do it on the kitchen table, and so on. And as for the positions—they can range from the ridiculous to the impossible, to the downright dangerous. Most of us can't even begin to understand what goes into them, let alone perform them.

But consider this—what is the main ingredient of any sexual position? It is the thrust. Vary the thrust and you vary the experience.

The length, the pleasure and the effectiveness of sex depends on the artistry of the thrusts.

Regardless of geography and position, sex can only come alive with the thrust.

The ancient love texts suggest an equal number of thrusting styles for women and men both. The different styles and pace of thrusting prescribed in the *Kama Sutra* are for the start of sex, so as to stimulate you to the right level of arousal. Once you are in the throes of passion and approaching orgasm there is no thought for rules and styles—your body and your instincts take over.

There can be many different ways of thrusting—the combinations are endless. How you thrust will set the tone for your lovemaking. And if you choose to start in a different way each time, or at least often enough, it will get your partner panting in anticipation and wondering each time what you will do next.

As we've seen, the erotic nerves and erogenous zones inside the vulva are located on different sides and at different depths and connect to various points in the body, which gives each spot its own sensations. So if you want an entirely new feeling, something other than what you normally feel, it's time to approach these zones and spots differently.

Make sure your partner is extremely well lubricated. This will not only ensure that your partner feels no discomfort but will also reduce friction and help delay the orgasm.

The first thing to do is figure out how you generally enter your partner—the depth and the speed. If you are going to vary things you need to understand how you normally do it.

Men's thrusts

Thrust without entering. I want to start with this one because in terms of effectiveness on a scale of 1 to 10 this is a 20! Stay at the opening of the yoni and pulse back and forth without entering. There is a real romance to this thrust because, unlike regular sex, this doesn't need a change of position so you can stay face to face as well as maintain the cuddle.

Tip: Don't rush it—give it at least ten minutes. Use one hand to stay in place if necessary.

Enter but only just. This one takes some practice because the idea is to enter up to the first erogenous point which is immediately inside the lips of the yoni—no further and no less. Then move back and forth knocking against that point. This spot generally gets ignored during sex because of its location and because it has such little stimulation it is extremely sensitive and can provide incredible pleasure.

Tip: Lie on your side facing each other, be comfortable because, at least initially, you will need to use your hands to manoeuvre yourself.

The 'no touch' thrust. Time to multitask. Using your fingers, very slowly open and close the lips of the yoni while thrusting against the side of your partner's thigh. The opening of the lips allows air to enter which is always a little bit colder than the inside of the yoni and this meeting of temperatures causes an unusual sensation that makes the yoni muscles pulsate. Most women will tell you that this is one of the most exciting sensations they have ever felt. This is best done with the upper part of the body almost upright—on the sofa or propped up against a lot of pillows. Her body should be facing forward, you should be to her left (so that you can use the left hand) and slightly on your side.

Tip: Do this for a minimum of ten minutes. It takes time to build up.

Creating a vacuum. Extremely slowly, enter all the way in, as deep as you can go so that you fill her completely and there is nothing there but you—not even air. Then pull back to the edge, but not out. From here on just do short, shallow thrusts at the entrance. The vacuum will make her want to pull you back inside.

Tip: Don't break contact.

Pulsing. Enter all the way in, as deep as you can go. Press

your body into your partner's and go in all the way to the end. Then just stay there and pulse. This is one of the most difficult thrusts for a man to practise because with this position it takes a great deal to hold back the ejaculation—this kind of thrust is calculated to make a man lose control. But on the other hand it is also one of the most exciting for women. The entire yoni is filled, which causes her tremendous excitement. The base (the glans) of the phallus rubs against the clitoris while the front nudges the erogenous spots that are deep inside.

Women's thrusts

As a woman you too can be a decision maker on the thrusts—albeit in a different way. The simplest way to take control is to decide how to position yourself. You can use a variety of cushion shapes—round, square, rectangular, crescent shaped—which when placed under different parts of your body will change the angle of your yoni and how your partner accesses it. Even the slightest tilt can make a difference to the sensations.

You can also change the angle and depth of penetration by placing your legs on different parts of your partner's body. Lie flat and place your feet on his shoulders, lift your bottom and link your ankles around his back, bend your knees and place your feet on his hips. This will define the thrust according to your desire.

If you place your calves on his shoulders you will get the deepest penetration.

If you want to keep the thrusts shallow, ball up your fists and place them on either side of your groin—this will limit penetration. Keep it going with the hands in place for some time and then, when he is least expecting it, remove your fists and let him plunge all the way in.

Keep it exciting for yourself. Change from one to the other as you want. Arch or flatten your back in the middle of things, move your feet from one position to the other. Everything changes the nature of the thrust.

Vatsyayan explains in his introduction to the *Kama Sutra* that all the techniques and instructions that he offers in the book are either to help people build up their passion or for people of low sexual drive who will never really get to the point of heightened passion and need instruction on what to do to satisfy their partners.

However, it's important to understand that using different types of thrusts will take a lot of work to perfect.

It needs strength and rhythm—you need a strong back and lots of energy to maintain the thrusts for any length of time as well as to be able to hold yourself back from orgasming too soon. Thrusts should be like the notes of a musical compositions—smooth and varied, like the brilliance of an orchestra. Jerky and uncoordinated thrusting is painfully unfulfilling and unsexy.

My Advice

Angles—a very simple and effective way to change the thrusts is to change the angle of penetration. Thrust from side to side instead of back and forth. Enter only halfway and aim to hit the middle of the yoni with each thrust rather than the end. This is where two of the major erotic nerves, the Sati and the Asati, are situated; these connect to the waist and the navel—the ones that will give you 'butterflies in your stomach'. Try it either fast or slow. Each one has its own advantages. Use different shapes of cushions under yourself or your partner. The *Kama Sutra* says one must have eight different shapes of cushions in the bedroom. Different shapes change the angle of penetration in a subtle way and make an impact. Putting them under different parts of the body—or equally removing them (like the pillow from under your head)—can change the thrust and the sensations.

Music—one of the most fabulous ways to thrust. Pick a piece of music and move to it. This saves you having to make decisions, to try and work out when to go deep or shallow, fast or slow. I always recommend classical music rather than popular music because the range is so much wider.

Speed—alternating fast and slow thrusts are another easy and effective way to add variety. It's not about a great and complicated array of techniques—just a little change can make all the difference.

Pillow Talk

In the village of Sangam lived a hot-tempered soldier called Raja and his very beautiful but immoral wife, Rukmini. One day, when they were out at a festival, Raja noticed his wife making eyes at a very handsome stranger—they were exchanging notes in the secret lover's code. The soldier was so angry he dragged Rukmini back to the house where he beat her soundly and then locked her up indoors and told her that from that day on she could not set foot outside without him beside her. Rukmini was so furious with him that she decided she would pay him back by having sex with her lover right under his nose. She sent her lover a message which said 'outside my house is a big banyan tree. Tonight, dig a trench, the size of your body, in the ground under the tree and then lie down in it with your manhood erect.' At the appointed hour, she ran outside and, squatting on top of her hidden lover, she called out to her husband. 'You are so good with the bow and arrow, why don't you shoot me down a moonbeam.' The solider was eager to please his wife back into good humour, so he shot one useless arrow after the other at the moon while she laughed delightedly each time and continued till she had had her pleasure....

---

*Most of the stories in this chapter have been adapted from the *Sukasaptati*, edited and translated by Pt Ramakanta Tripathi, published by Chaukhamba Sanskrit Pratishthan.

The *Kama Sutra* says that you must tell your lover stories, before and after sex, to create the mood. It was the man's role to tell these stories, to seduce and pleasure the beloved. Before sex the stories should be naughty, gossipy and suggestive to arouse and excite and get the juices flowing. They could be reminiscences—'remember when we went to such-and-such place I did this to you', etc. to make them blush or feel aroused with the memory of the event. They could be gossipy stories that would make the woman giggle and join in. If she was very shy and very nervous, the man would tell stories of how beautiful women are very wicked and how the poor men don't stand a chance—these were calculated to make her gasp in indignation and deny these accusations. The idea was to get a reaction. You picked the stories according to the character of the person you were with. It was a great technique—the man was talking to her the whole time so his attention was entirely on her, and the purpose was to entertain her and make her forget her inhibitions, so that by the time he was ready to start kissing her in earnest, she was in the right frame of mind.

The king's minister had a beautiful but adulterous wife called Kalavati. One day as she was giving her husband a bath she saw her lover walk past on the street outside, at the prearranged time, on his way to their favourite rendezvous. Kalavati said, 'Oh, oh, the wind is blowing my scarf down the road' and ran off to meet her lover. She spent a long time with him—what was the point if you weren't going to satisfy yourself fully—but now she had to explain to her husband what had taken her away for so long in the middle of his bath. So she climbed down the well and began to yell for help. Everyone thought the poor woman had fallen in and when she was rescued, the husband took her back home full of solicitous concern for her wellbeing.

On the other hand, after-sex stories had to be sweet and romantic, of happy endings and successful romances, to make your lover feel secure, happy and cherished. What you say and how you say it will determine the mood of your lover and the quality of the sexual experience.

After the exertions of the picnic when she (the most beloved) fell asleep on his shoulder the king had his servants cut off the sleeve of his beautifully brocaded jacket so that he wouldn't disturb her rest.

And with all the weird and wonderful positions that the *Kama Sutra* is most renowned for, all the strange traditions of love scratches and the detailed explanations of oral sex, this is the most revolutionary tool of seduction in the *Kama Sutra*—communication. The conversation, the teasing, the give and take of ideas, the hide and seek of all of your fantasies—the stories that you tell each other. Utterly obvious to the masters 2,000 years ago and yet what most of us in the twenty-first century still haven't understood is just how important communicating is to your sexual success.

The level of excitement with which your lover approaches having sex with you depends on the banter, the chat, the flirtation, the mental stimulation, the frisson of the verbal battle that has gone on just before—that's what really gets the juices flowing. And the eagerness with which they return to your bed again—that too depends on how it was for them the last time.

When I say 'before and after', I mean the absolute beginning (at the start of foreplay) and the absolute end (after the orgasm).

Sex itself is generally more blurred, what we remember vividly however is the build-up—the arousal, the mounting excitement and even more, the calm down—was it the gradual 'sigh-worthy' simmering down of a delightful experience or was it the sudden thump of an anti-climax (which is the fate of most excitement).

This is what colours our idea of the sexual experience and is extremely important. If the 'before' is good, the sex will be fabulous, if the 'after' is brilliant, it will lay the groundwork for next time—the 'end' is just the beginning of the next time.

As a man, how do you begin foreplay? Do you just jump into it—you have your partner with you, you know it's going to end in sex so let's just go at it? And how do you finish? Do you have an après-sex routine? Or do you feel that you've done lots beforehand, and now is your chance to roll over and go to sleep while your partner washes herself?

The *Kama Sutra* says that the success of the before and after depends on really good communication—what you talk about and the degree of attentiveness.

But what is good conversation? Is it a chat about politics or the latest film, the state of the economy or the latest fashion? Should one talk about war or about music? Is it true that to keep a man interested the woman must always be the listener; she must let the man talk about his interests and pretend to be enthusiastic about it? And then again what constitutes attentiveness—who determines what degree of attention is suitable? Also, emotions and energies differ vastly before and after sex—so how should the attention change?

It's the Venus and Mars syndrome!

Even more importantly, is the same conversation 'good' before sex as well as after sex?

The *Kama Sutra* has the answer.

Vatsyayan translates the idea of good conversation into stories. Tell your lover stories.

Storytelling is one of the sixty-four essential skills of the *Kama Sutra*. Not only did it mark you at as a man of substance and breeding—it showed that you were well versed in literature and the arts—but it was also a brilliant tool of seduction because you would know exactly what to say to keep your beloved amused and interested.

And it instructs the man on exactly what kind of stories to narrate—what is arousing, what is exciting, what will help shed her inhibitions, what will overcome shyness and embarrassment, what will make your lover feel cherished.

Before and after stories were different because you were looking to create a different mood, to arouse different emotions.

Before foreplay is the time to create an atmosphere for sex—to amuse, excite, arouse, to get rid of any inhibitions and shyness, to get your lover panting for your first touch. After sex you need to create a mood of contentment and happiness.

The start of foreplay and post orgasm are very delicate moments, women are usually more nervous at this time and their emotions are more fragile, so the onus of getting the balance right is on the man. Vatsyayan says that the man must make conversation that will entertain the woman—with the emphasis on 'entertaining'. This is not the time for the man to share his office woes or pontificate on his political views.

According to Vatsyayan, of all the different types of stories, the best kind were the gossipy ones, the ones that made you laugh out loud. Happy moods are ideal for lovemaking. They say happiness was Cleopatra's seduction mantra because if a man associated you with his happiest moments, he would never want to leave you. To laugh together while making love, or waking up in the morning and laughing with your partner, made you an irresistible lover.

Malathi had not seen her lover in several days so that night she invited him to her bed. 'My husband sleeps on my right so get into the bed from the left side and make love to me from behind. Come after midnight, he'll be asleep by then.' But just as the lover started the husband turned around in his sleep and caught the lover's manhood by mistake. Thinking that he had caught a thief he started to shout for help—'Malathi I have caught a thief. Go quickly and find a candle while I hold him.' But Malathi told him that he should go get the candle and she would hold the thief. By the time he came back the lover had disappeared and Malathi was on the bed holding a leather strap which she said the dog had brought in. Happy that they were safe the husband went back to sleep.

The *Kama Sutra* says that after sex, the lovers should put some distance between themselves briefly. They should go to different bathrooms to wash. It advises against the couple bathing and washing together after sex—a brief separation is necessary because after orgasm there is a dispersal of energy that can cause a disconnect and can lead to emotional distance. This disconnect needs to be healed. So one should bathe and wash separately, and after bathing and getting into fresh clothes, the couple must come together one more time where the man must practice attentiveness and good conversation.

Taking her to the terrace (if it is too hot indoors), he must arrange a nice dinner of an assortment of dishes—the *Kama Sutra* says there should be kebabs, vegetables, breads, different types of sweets and chicken broth (this was particularly recommended as an energizing dish for tired courtesans, to recoup their strength after sex). He must offer her a drink and hold the cup to her lips with his own hands. After she has finished eating he will place her head on his lap and show her the different constellations and point out the stars and tell her stories.

Showing the constellations (another of the sixty-four skills which will be touched upon later in the book) was about making astrological predictions—the man telling his lover how the stars were aligned for them and all obstacles removed from the path of their love.

Vatsyayan tells us that the evening begins when you invite the woman to your home. To show her how much you have been looking forward to her company, decorate the house with flowers, perfume the rooms etc. Her first impression should be of how beautiful everything looks. As the evening progresses, the surroundings will fade into the background but the perfume will remain in her subconscious as a memory of the night.

Drinks should be offered but the book is very particular that it should be no more than a couple of drinks—enough to shed a few inhibitions but not enough to make her drunk. Being drunk never leads to good sex.

Do not serve dinner—just a few small snacks. Food was to be consumed afterwards. Eating and drinking heavily beforehand leads to unsatisfactory sex. The body uses a lot of energy to digest the food and it also needs a lot of energy to get the sexual juices working—it can only do one thing at a time.

Sit near her but not next to her. Move closer to her gradually during the evening. The touching should be kept to a bare minimum to begin with—just a couple of feather light kisses dropped casually, a quick flick to her hair, brief touches to the edge of her sari—talking to her all the time, 'telling her your stories', making her laugh, while getting little bit closer and more intimate and so on, till finally she is ready for the kissing to begin.

It has to be very carefully done because, says the *Kama Sutra*, a woman will love a man who does not push intimacy on her too soon, but she needs to be completely aware how desperately he wants to do so. If he takes the time to arouse her, to indulge her hesitations, ostensibly holding his own desires in check, he will have won her heart for always.

How you behave after sex is even more important than your behaviour before. Before sex we are all heading towards excitement, there is a build-up of adrenaline and hormones, we know there is going to be a reward waiting at the end of it, therefore many of us are happy to work a lot harder to make it happen. After sex, there is a tendency to roll over and go to sleep because 'it's all over anyway'. For the time being you have had what you wanted, one can deal with 'next time' when you get to next time.

However, the *Kama Sutra* says that the man who can understand the importance of après-sex stories is the lover of every woman's dreams. This is the time to be even more communicative, to show even more attention and caring.

When the beautiful dancers arrived to entertain the party, the beloved burst into uncontrollable tears. If the king saw these young beauties eventually he would leave her for one of them. To show how much he loved her, the king passed a law—no one was allowed to introduce more beauties to him and anyone who did would be executed.

The book tells us that unlike with men, for women orgasm is not a stand-alone experience. It's what happens after orgasm that decides the quality of the orgasm. If the woman is cuddled and made to feel loved and wanted it becomes pleasurable for her, if she is ignored afterwards or left to herself it becomes an unsatisfactory experience.

In the mountains lived a girl so beautiful that everyone who saw her went mad with desire. Even the sage Narada lost his head over her. But he was so angry with his own reaction that he cursed the girl, 'just as she makes us all feel crazy with desire she will also lose herself and commit adultery one day'. But when he calmed down and he realized he had been unfair he lessened the curse a little— 'she will not however be blamed for her adultery and her husband will not abandon her for it'. In keeping with the curse, one day when the girl was lying naked by the lake after her bath, a wandering demigod saw her and, struck by her beauty, disguised himself as her husband and had sex with her. Just then her husband came back unexpectedly and finding her in the mellow state of pleasure that comes after a fulfilling orgasm he knew right away that she had been unfaithful. He was furious. He pulled out his sword—she deserved to die! But before he could strike her the goddess herself came out of a rock and stopped him. She told him about the curse—it wasn't the girl's fault, it was destined. The husband's doubts were set to rest and he hugged his wife and took her back home where they lived happily ever after.

My Advice

After sex is the time to make your lover feel loved. It's the time to lay the foundation for the next sexual encounter. Being more attentive and loving after sex means you get more brownie points for the same amount of effort and will have your lover waiting impatiently for next time.

Another name for Kamadeva is Smara or Memory. Memories can be happy and pleasurable or full of anger and discontent, and this will impact all future lovemaking. It could bring your lover back to your bed in an excited frame of mind, wanting to be with you, it could chase them away altogether or (if they are stuck with you and have to come back to your bed) it could bring back a reluctant lover. The power of the subconscious mind is tremendous. Not only will it impact this relationship, it will also colour all other sexual relationships, so it is very important to get this right.

No relationship survives without effective communication and sex needs constant freshening up to stay exciting.

The *Kama Sutra* has hit the nail on the head when it says that great conversation is the ultimate tool of seduction. It recognized 2,000 years ago, in a society of culturally well versed men, at a time when men agreed that seduction was an art form, that communication between lovers is a fragile thing, difficult to understand at the best of times and not a skill that everyone has.

And so Vatsyayan developed a formula—stories—a manner of communication that would meet all the diverse demands of occasion and character.

Does that all sound like a lot of work?

They say a woman loves a man who will not try to bypass the seduction process, a man who will not hurry her into sex even though he really wants to, someone who will take the time to arouse and excite her even if his own desires are really intense—that is the man who will win her in the end.

Paan and the Arts of Seduction

Paan is a wrap made with betel leaf and areca nut (not betel nut, as is the common misconception). It is a delicacy generally found in Eastern cultures, particularly in India. In modern times, it is a breath freshener to be eaten after a meal—but in the time of the *Kama Sutra* this little nut wrapped up in a leaf was so much more.

Paan, says the *Kama Sutra*, was the transition between foreplay and sex. It was the very last thing that was offered in the games of foreplay—when the beloved felt she was fully aroused; after she had been kissed, caressed, embraced, love-bitten to her heart's content—she offered her lover paan. It meant she was ready for sex.

If, on the other hand, the beloved was an inexperienced and hesitant lover then the *Kama Sutra* advised that the man could offer the paan instead. He was to take a bite out of the betel leaf and offer the rest of it to her. This would be the first feel of his lips on hers. If she took the paan from him, it meant she was ready to accept his kisses.

Paan was the ultimate symbol of romance and passion in the history of seduction and there was an entire erotic vocabulary centred around the giving and taking of it—everything that you could dream of and more. Both men and women used paan to send messages—in the absence of text messages and emojis one used paan to communicate with one's lover. If you wanted to begin flirting, there was a paan for it, if you wanted to romance a lover, there was a paan for it, if you wanted to seduce an ex back—there was a paan for it.

The nuance, the subtlety and the degree of seduction that this tiny little betel leaf could conjure up was as unbelievable as it was delightful—it was seductive without being graphic, delicate without being too subtle, fun without being loud and thoroughly suggestive without being explicit. It was a time when people understood that there was more to seduction than 'swipe left, swipe right'!

Let us begin with the paans of invitation.

'Desperately in love'—if you wanted to tell someone you were desperately in love with them you would send what the *Kama Sutra* calls the Kaushal paan. The Kaushal paan had to be made with quantifiable perfection. Each condiment in it had to be placed in its precise spot next to the other; nothing could be placed on top of anything else. The quantity of each ingredient had to be exact. Instead of the sweet paste, one had to use catechu (kathha). Finally, each fold had to be turned down with mathematical precision. This type of paan would be wrapped in four red threads and could only be carried to the lover by a wandering monk. Any lack in the paan would be seen as a lack in love and the lover would be spurned out of hand.

'Setting up a date'—to 'hook' someone for a night of passion you sent an Ankush paan. This paan was shaped like an isosceles triangle with the top corner bent to resemble a hook.

'I am feverish with excitement at the thought of seeing

you'—a Kandarp paan was sent. This was shaped like an equilateral triangle and could only be delivered in the evenings after the moon had risen.

'I want to sleep with you'—a rectangular paan (the shape of a single bed) was delivered by a very trusted servant. Many a heart has been broken because the person delivering it managed to seduce the lover for themselves!

And, of course, love messages are not one-sided. Lovers must respond as well.

'Sorry I don't have the time to see you'—Chaturstra, a square paan.

'I don't love you'—a paan without the supari (areca nut).

'I love you'—a paan with cardamom.

'I have absolutely no interest in you, don't contact me again'—the paan had to be made inside out (with the dark side of the leaf on the inside) and then tied with black thread. A black thread at any time was a sign of rejection and would have been enough to strike fear into the heart of the lover. But added to that an inside-out paan—the lover might as well be dead!

'I am ready to sleep with you'—two small triangular paans joined at the mouth and tied together with red thread.

'I get excited telling you in public that I want to sleep with you'—the paan for this message is the same as the one above, but now imagine that you are in a crowded place—close enough to see each other but separated by the crowds. You would put one paan in your mouth, and taking the second one, you would touch your mouth to it and then make a gesture in the air as if offering it to your beloved. It was as intimate and arousing as a physical touch.

'I am breaking up with you'—this one was positively brutal. You sent a paan that was torn in the middle and tied with black thread.

Seema Anand

'I am ready to spend my life with you'—a paan tied in red cloth.

'To express overwhelming love'—this was a step further than 'desperate love'—you sent the aforementioned Kaushal paan but with even more precision. The paan had to be filled with supari that had been chopped into little bits and then stuck together again with sticky paste. Saffron was added to the centre and the outside was coated in sandalwood paste.

'To get rid of dinner guests'—cinnamon-scented paan. You have spent the evening in the company of your beloved surrounded by other people—tantalizingly close and yet so far. You have exchanged glances, short conversations, perhaps a quick touch in passing till finally all you can think of is your bodies entangled together in the heat of passion. When you reach this point you offer your guests paan heavily scented with cinnamon. Your guests will get the hint and leave!

'Let's end foreplay and begin sex'—when every erotic nerve in her body is tingling, when her breath is short and her love juices are flowing, when she feels she is aroused and desperately needs to feel her lover inside her, she offers him a paan filled with a combination of valerian, jackfruit, camphor, cardamom and cloves, stuck together with ginger paste.

'I am a below average lover and I need help'—yes, there was even a paan for inept lovers, for men who didn't have the ability to satisfy a woman properly, for whatever reason. A paan made with quince was offered to the beloved. Quince is a highly aromatic fruit, a cross between a pear and a guava and with a reputation for being a love potion. It was said that this could bring a woman to orgasm very quickly no matter how rapacious she was, thereby saving the lover the embarrassment of trying to bring her to arousal through means that he was obviously not very capable of. She would leave fully satisfied and his reputation would stay intact.

In ancient Greece quince was offered at the altar of Aphrodite. In ancient Rome there was a law that made it necessary for all newly married couples to eat quince before consummating their marriage in order to avoid disappointment and the potential breakup of the relationship. And in ancient India it was used to save the reputations of men who lacked the ability to satisfy a woman properly by feeding it to the women—the paan would work its magic where the man couldn't. It was especially given to women who had overly large vulvas.

(A paan shop in the Indian town of Aurangabad claims to have a paan that can turn any man into a superlative lover—and unlike Viagra it has an effect that can last up to several days! The paan costs the equivalent of sixty pounds, a cost that the proprietor justifies by the extraordinarily expensive and unusual ingredients he claims it contains. But the magic touch is a secret ingredient which only he knows—and his customers swear by it. They say it is especially bought by men for their wedding days. I wonder if the secret ingredient is quince.)

There were even paans made with crushed gems. According to one source, sapphires would be crushed and served in paan. Sapphires are associated with the capricious and often malevolent demigod Shani and so they have to be worn with enormous care, but if they suit you then you could have the neelamani paan (made with crushed sapphires). It would remove all negative sexual energies.

The vocabulary of the betel leaf was as extensive as it was complex.

For example, the end-of-foreplay paan was traditionally offered by the woman—it was her decision as to when foreplay should finish and sex could begin. It was a very overt act—she would step back flushed and sweating with passion, breathless with desire, allowing her lover to see her in all her arousal, coy and inviting, confident that she was in control and she would make the paan. Occasionally, however, the man could also take the lead in offering paan to bring foreplay to a close. The new lover (or new wife) may be very shy and lack the confidence to stop and make the paan. If she wasn't quite confident, the man was advised to make the paan and place it on her lap—it would save her the embarrassment of making it, all she had to do was to pick it up and offer it to him.

An even more delicate permutation of this custom was where, taking into account her inexperience and hesitation, the lover took a bite of the paan and offered the rest to her so she could get used to the idea of feeling his lips on hers. If she took his paan it meant she was ready accept his kisses.

It was like writing a love letter. Depending on what you put inside the paan, how you fragranced it, how you tied it, even the lac with which you sealed the package carrying the paan—everything had its own special meaning. Each shape or filling or even the way it was delivered could create any mood that the lover may have wished for, from romance to rejection to coquetry to outright invitation.

With one type of paan you could tell your beloved that you wanted to worship at her feet forever, with another you could tell your lover that you didn't like him and he shouldn't call again, yet another could mean you wanted sex with no strings attached, while a slightly different one could be to beg for just one little kiss to tide you over while you waited patiently for something more!

Both men and women practised the giving and taking of paan.

For sexual purposes, it was generally given with the left hand. The beloved in the act of giving paan to end foreplay is known as 'priyatama vamhast' or 'she who offers paan with the left hand' because sex was an activity for the left hand. Eating and praying was done with the right hand, sex and all things sexual were performed with the left hand.

My Advice

With its subtle and evocative vocabulary, paan has been the language of lovers for over 2,000 years. Artists and poets have used it to depict love and lovemaking—now it's your turn. And the great news is that it can still be practised. It doesn't need special circumstances, private spaces or acrobatic positions and yet it is guaranteed to add a touch of romance and spice to any relationship.

Let your imagination have a field day. If the *Kama Sutra* thought it was the ultimate art of seduction it is definitely worth trying.

Add spice to your love life—practise sending messages through paan. It can be a fun way to form a connection or start a flirtation. Innovate.

Get creative. There is a shop in southern India that sells fifty-one different types of paan. Imagine what you could do with them.

The next time you have guests over, serve paan—of different shapes and with different messages for your guests to choose from.

Look for paintings or poetry with paan analogies—use this as a conversation piece with your lover. Let this be a shared interest that leads to a closer bond.

Inexplicably, there is something supremely sexy about a woman who carries a small silver box or a silk pouch of supari. Not a packet of chewing gum or polo mints or a little foil packet—a beautiful silver box with good quality and unusual supari. Pull this out at social gatherings and offer some around. It attracts a lot of attention.

Try all of the above. Let sensuality into your blood stream.

Today in India we associate the elaborate paan customs with the Mughal court and the aristocratic and polite societies of Hyderabad and Lucknow.

But the tradition of paan existed in India centuries before the Mughals made an appearance. Not only that—but as we know from the *Kama Sutra*—it existed in all its luxurious sensuousness.

As we set off exploring the arts of seduction, let paan be the first stop.

Sex and Food

According to ancient wisdom a big, heavy meal before sex is not a good idea—all the energy of the body gets channelled into the digestive process and leaves none for sexual arousal. The body needs a great deal of steam to digest the meal as well as raise sexual energy and, unfortunately, it will automatically pick the digestion process—you don't get to decide.

Food should be had *after* sex. The *Kama Sutra* recommends that after sex the man should offer the beloved a beautifully presented gourmet meal, with varied flavours to satisfy her taste buds. Before sex one should stick to light savoury snacks and a couple of drinks—literally two drinks because being drunk reduces the erection and is not conducive to great sex.

Sex needs energy, good sex needs a lot of energy, fabulous sex needs huge amounts of energy. Food and drink should help in the process, not distract from it.

In the time of the *Kama Sutra* the social norm was to eat during the mid-afternoon. Whether one was preparing for sex or not, eating later in the evening (our dinner time) was not generally recommended.

Ideally, if the couple had a date for sex (and both partners were aware of it), the man would feed the beloved a few light snacks before they made love. Something warm—because it takes less energy to digest. Not fatty meat—this gives sweat and sexual fluids an unpleasant odour during sex. Nuts were often included—the good fatty acids in nuts give extra blood flow to the genitals and raise the sexual energy properly.

After sex was the time to spoil her with every kind of delicacy to please her taste buds. The aprés sex meal was to include mutton soup (as I've mentioned, courtesans had to be fed mutton soup and chicken broth to recoup their energies after an exhausting night), kebabs, grilled food, vegetables, fragrant rice, walnuts, mangoes, candied oranges and other sweets.

And, the *Kama Sutra* says, it was not just what you offered her to eat but *how* you offered it. The lover was to pick up each item of food, bite into it first and then offer it to her, telling her 'this one is sweet, this one is salty'. He must offer her a variety of juices and sherbets, holding the cup to her lips with his hands.

If, however, food before sex was unavoidable—you had invited her to a party and heavy food and drink was consumed—then a couple of hours gap and some physical activity was necessary. The *Kama Sutra* stipulates that after dinner, guests should be entertained with cock and quail fights, singing games (antakshri etc.) and other activities. Digestives and mouth fresheners such as paan should also be offered. All this would give the digestive process time to settle down and make the body 'love' ready again.

The passage of time and wishful thinking have developed a long list of the 'right' kind of foods—aphrodisiacs—to eat to become virile and sexy.

The *Kama Sutra* (and all the love texts of the ancient East) insists that the foods you eat make all the difference to your sexual prowess, not because they have magical properties but because they work with the organs in individual ways to release energy and increase blood flow.

The best kind of aphrodisiac was simply right eating! Good sex needed a lot of energy. Eating right meant good digestion, good digestion meant good metabolism and good metabolism meant lots of energy—if your body was lacking in energy you were not going to be any good at sex! If you were going to flop into a breathless heap after a few minutes then all skills of seduction and all knowledge of the erotic arts were pointless.

One of the most popular aphrodisiacs was a mixture of scented water and honey because it was a great cure for constipation. Constipation causes genital odours and energy blockages—both were death to good sex.

Fish was also an excellent food for lovers. Not just oysters—almost any kind of fish. The ancients believed that fish expelled trapped wind and reduced bloating—getting rid of wind was the quickest way to unblock the channels of sexual energy. Fish also generated heat in the body which in turn made you more passionate. So strong was this belief in the efficacy of fish as an aphrodisiac that men of the British East India Company held that having sex with Bengali women (a fish-eating community) was the only way to beat the unbearable monsoon heat which was known to completely sap people of energy. According to an article that appeared in a London newspaper in the 1800s, the Company men (back in the time of Jahangir) had even applied to the Mughal emperor for permission to have sex with Bengali women during the monsoons—for health reasons.

The zinc in almonds boosts the male sex hormones and the ancients believed that their fragrance was a turn-on for women. Romans used almond confetti during weddings (like many Indian communities throw rice) and, according to the

Bible, Samson wooed Delilah with almond branches.

Alcohol was great but in moderation. A couple of glasses not only lowered inhibitions and relaxed you but added to the beauty of the woman as well—'flushed cheeks', 'red eyes', 'wine breath' were high compliments. Too much wine however caused people to perspire and flop all over their lovers. Vatsyayan begins by saying that 'abstinence is a very special virtue' (amadyapa iti nagrakagunah) but moderation was a good compromise. Generally the alcohol referred to in the *Kama Sutra* was a form of red wine—one, because it was a warm drink and, second, because red was the colour of passion and anything red was considered an aphrodisiac. It was perfumed with lotus flowers or new mango leaves—to counter the effects of bad breath.

Paan was a very popular aphrodisiac. It served a variety of purposes. It freshened the breath, it beautified the mouth (staining the lips red) and the different ingredients were supposed to have their own particular effect on the senses. Besides which, the love vocabulary associated with the giving and taking of paan made it even more desirable.

Sugarcane juice and sali rice come highly recommended. Legend has it that when the Sun god was drinking his share of the Amrit (the nectar of immortality) a few drops fell to the ground and these became sugarcane juice and sali rice. Sugarcane derived its aphrodisiac reputation from the season (it's hot) and the taste (sweet foods were associated with sweetening the senses). Sali rice comes in different varieties—one has a lotus fragrance, one is red and there is even a variety that looks like the male organ and was considered a great aphrodisiac (the Indian tradition of throwing rice at newly-weds comes from sali rice). Whatever their reality both things are great because for some reason they help mellow the senses.

Virgil wrote that rocket leaf (arugula) salad was good for

the libido because 'it excites the sexual desire of drowsy people'.

Onions, garlic and meat increase the heat in the blood. In ancient India widows and women whose husbands were travelling were not permitted to eat any of these foods for fear of arousing passion.

Condiments like turmeric, red chillies, black pepper etc. were considered very effective stimulants because they cleared the blood stream and made digestion easier.

The Chinese believed that foods that are good for the kidneys are the best aphrodisiacs because the kidney is the organ that balances the energy of the genitals. According to Chinese medicine, the kidneys like foods that have deep colours and are naturally salty. They suggest a diet of fish (sea fish are better than river fish), black mushrooms, black beans, blueberries, eggs (especially quail's eggs), red meat (not chicken), bone marrow, walnuts and tofu.

My Advice

It's time to understand what makes you tick.

We all like the idea of using something to help us—it makes us feel more secure. It's not a bad thing so long as you understand that aphrodisiacs are not magic potions. At best, certain foods will enhance your performance a little, they won't change you into a gifted and powerful lover. Even Viagra will simply give you a long-lasting erection, not the physical energy to sustain sexual activity—an unending hard-on is not the same as being able to do something with it.

Food has all sorts of properties—some real, some imagined. Casanova used to eat celery before a night of seduction—he believed it was an aphrodisiac and that was enough to make it one.

Somewhere in the world and at some point in time every food has probably been an aphrodisiac. The ancients believed that food that resembled the genitals had the properties of genitals—mangoes, figs, etc. because they look like breasts; avocados, shellfish, etc. that resemble the vagina; gourds, cucumbers, bananas because they are shaped like the penis.

Foods that had to be 'licked' were the voyeur's aphrodisiac—particularly the extra juicy fruits, like mangoes and watermelon.

Anything red was an aphrodisiac because red is the colour of passion—strawberries, watermelon, beetroot. Even rubies were powdered and mixed with honey or goat's milk and were believed to have great aphrodisiac properties on the proviso that they had to be secretly administered, that is, without the knowledge of the person consuming the food.

Rhino horn had its reputation simply because of its shape which resembles an erect phallus. However there is nothing even remotely aphrodisiac about it. It is made up entirely of keratin and eating it is no different than biting your own nails.

Scientifically speaking, none of these were of any real use. They were what we believed them to be and that's what worked for us.

The best sex comes with a healthy body and an energized mind and food only adds to this fantastic experience.

The *Kama Sutra* says that when feeding your lover the presentation and the variety is extremely important. Today you have it all—beautifully presented dishes, fabulously written menus, the restaurant's decor, the fragrance, their choice of music—they're all potential aphrodisiacs. You have so much to choose from—don't limit yourself to old ideas of magic potions.

A healthy diet will open up the channels of your sexual energy and regular exercise will give you the stamina to stay with it longer.

Don't have a heavy meal before sex—it doesn't lead to good sex. If you have had too much to eat or drink the sex will just not match up to the expectations of the evening.

Too much alcohol slows down the sexual energy and makes the erection more difficult to sustain.

There is no such thing as the perfect aphrodisiac—the perfect aphrodisiac changes with age. At every stage your needs are different and so is the thing that will fulfil those needs.

As you get older you feel you are slowing down, you can't do the things you could before and need something to boost your drive as well as your sexual prowess. The thing to remember is that change is not a bad thing, slower doesn't mean that your sexual drive is diminished and older doesn't mean you have lost it altogether. It's different—and with that so is the way that you respond to pleasure.

Savour your food and your sex at each stage. It's a new experience.

If I were to choose one effective aphrodisiac I would pick foods that contain zinc, such as apples, asparagus and pumpkin seeds. And as a placebo aphrodisiac, I would pick paan—I think it would be very exciting to be seduced by paan.

Therapeutic Sex

The premise is simple. Sexual energy is the most powerful form of energy that the body can produce but generally it all just dissipates with the orgasm. Imagine, however, if you could use this energy for your own benefit.

During sex all the metabolic processes of the entire body are activated, every single organ goes through some form of change. There is a change in respiration, in the heartbeat, the circulation, the brain waves, and every gland and organ starts to secrete some or the other hormone.

Everything metabolizes during sex to produce an energy so powerful that it can create life.

Just like if you were to take a bottle and fill it with water and make the water flow in whichever direction you turned the bottle, similarly, Ayurveda believes that you can use different sexual positions to make sexual energy flow in different ways and heal yourself. With specific positions you can focus the flow of the energy to reach certain points, to heal and strengthen specific parts of the body.

The underlying principle of therapeutic sex, as it's described in the ancient erotic texts, was control. The positions had to be held for long periods of time. Movements, breath, even the time of day had to be very carefully regulated; ejaculation was to be stringently controlled. Therapeutic sex was not about orgasm or even pleasure, it was about harnessing, holding and directing sexual energy. And according to the texts, this energy could heal everything from low haemoglobin to gastric wind and bloating to back pain.

Here are a few positions to start practising.

The first thing to master is the rhythm of thrusting.

Everything from the length, the pleasure and the effectiveness of the sexual act depends on the artistry of the thrusts. How the man thrusts will define which erotic nerves are stimulated inside the vulva which in turn will decide what kind of energy will arise and how it will travel. It also increases the man's staying power—the right kind of thrusting can help him control ejaculation and increase the variety of what he can do in bed.

The most important thing to remember—for therapeutic sex, thrusts should be done very, very slowly. Ideally, they should be combinations of shallow and deep thrusts and done in sequences of ten.

Begin with nine shallow thrusts followed by one deep one. When you have mastered that move on to eight shallow and two deep, and so on, until you can manage one shallow and nine deep thrusts. According to Taoist philosophy the art of thrusting should be learnt and practised as one would a musical instrument, because you need to master it with the same expertise.

In therapeutic sex, unlike normal sex, there is to be no foreplay.

Begin each position immediately with penetration and spend time on regular thrusting (like in normal sex) to get the rhythm going and to get all the processes of the body working. It is essential that the woman be lubricated artificially and thoroughly to avoid discomfort. Once the organs, glands and hormones heat up, the specific positions can be performed. There should be no kissing during therapeutic sex.

Position 1

This position is meant to improve the concentration of semen in the man as well as cure internal bleeding in the woman—the word 'bleeding' here refers to heat draining out of the abdominal area of the woman. This position will address a number of problems—infertility, lack of energy and blood flow.

This position requires two sets of ten thrusts at a time. Start with nine shallow, one deep and gradually increase the number of deep thrusts every day.

The woman should lie on her right side, legs spread wide. The man lies on his left, full length alongside her, between her legs.

The man must do one sequence of ten thrusts, very slowly, and then lie inside the woman for about twenty minutes. During this time the man should remain totally still while the woman makes very slight rotational movements with the pelvis only—no other part of her should move. The breathing should be centred in the lower abdomen—it is important for both partners to focus and centre the breathing carefully.

At the end of the twenty minutes the man should do another ten thrusts and then once again lie still inside the woman before bringing the lovemaking to an end.

If practised in the correct fashion, the flow of energy will begin at the top of the lungs and travel through to the spleen where it will circulate before flowing back to the top of the lungs.

This is to be practised every day for fifteen days, twice daily during the waxing half of the moon. There should be a period of at least seven hours between the two sessions.

Position 2

This position is practised in order to calm the mind and relieve stress. Interestingly, it was believed that for a man the stress relief was felt in the head and shoulders and for a woman it was felt by a calming of the sexual regions. This position was supposed to bring relief to both.

In this position, the woman lies on her back with her legs stretched out in front of her and her arms stretched out to the sides. She must have a rectangular cushion under her bottom—the shape of the cushion changes the angle at which the base of the spine is lifted and therefore changes the speed at which the energy flows.

The man should kneel in front of her, between her legs, keeping his back as straight as possible, because only in an upright position can you ensure the unrestricted passage of energy up to the head and a lying down position is best for the waves to spread to the lower abdomen.

This position is conducted with three sets of thrusts (nine+one) done one after the other. The entire process should take no less than ten minutes and no more than twenty.

After finishing, the man is advised to come out of the woman and lie beside her.

The movement of breath is very important in this position. The partners must breathe in through the nose and out through the mouth, very slowly and deeply and they must alternate the exhaling and the inhaling so that they are inhaling each other's breath. This is done in order to exchange energies and create a very intense focus, as in meditation.

The partners are asked to imagine the breath to be orange in colour and to physically visualize it entering and exiting the zones of stress. Interestingly, contrary to what we normally hear about clean air going in and unclean air coming out, the breath in this position had to be visualized as orange both going in and coming out because this was an exchange of energy. What one partner exhaled was being inhaled by the other—on a loop. So you were charging your breath with your own energy and offering it back to your partner.

This position was to be practised three times a day for twenty consecutive days, preferably in the spring or autumn as extremes of temperature are unsuitable to this position. The times of day are not specified but there had to be at least two hours between each session to digest the energy.

And finally—if at any point in this position you wished to culminate in an orgasm, it was not forbidden. Once you had followed all the instructions it was okay to finish any way you wanted.

There is some disagreement on the translations of how many times a day this position should be performed but do what you can—there should be no side effects.

Position 3

This position is said to help with the problem of stomach wind but it has far-reaching benefits. The ancients believed that gastric wind paralysed the internal organs and slowed down the functions of the whole body. Therefore, this position, by expelling wind, reinvigorated all the vital organs, including the sexual organs.

The woman must lie on her side (either side is okay but

left is better) and bend her legs. The man must lie at a right angle across her body and enter her vagina from behind. Note: even though he is entering from behind it is not in the anal canal, it is still 'regular' sex.

Four sets of ten thrusts are to be done and the rhythm is to be nine deep and one shallow only—this thrust pattern should not change. There is some debate as to whether it should be one set four times a day or four sets all at the same time. You should try what suits you best.

The thrusts should be very slow and the pace of the thrusting should match the breathing. Breathe in for the length of the inward thrust and breathe out as you pull out. This is a good way to control the pace of both the breath and the thrusts—if you feel one is getting faster control it with the other.

Practise it for twenty days at a stretch.

Position 4

Strengthening the joints.
The woman must lie on her right side. Stretching out her right leg very straight and long she must bend the left leg (which is on top) so that her body is partially twisted. The man must lie on top of her body supporting his weight on his own arms and penetrate her vagina.

This is done with a total of forty-five thrusts for a period of ten days. The first forty thrusts should be done in the same manner as the ones we have spoken of earlier—nine shallow, one deep, gradually changing to more deep ones. The last five are a little bit different.

These last five are all deep thrusts. With each thrust, as you penetrate all the way to the end of the vulva, keep the penis there and pulse slowly to the count of ten and then withdraw. Coordinate your breathing with the thrusts.

The varying positions and pressure of the thrusts stimulated an assortment of points which activated the electrical impulses, which in turn set different energy flows into motion. By keeping this energy rotating around the body with the help of your breath, blood flow and posture you channelled it into specific areas of the body to aid in its healing.

All of the above positions are based on stillness. Everything—breath, body, semen—had to be controlled in the same way as you would if you were meditating. Even the thrusts have to be done slowly and precisely in order to not disturb that stillness.

For men it was not just important to control their ejaculation, they had to learn how to 'injaculate'—to make the ejaculate travel back up inside their body instead of being expelled outside. Ejaculate (according to modern medical reports) contains a large percentage of the daily dose of nourishment for a man. If you were setting out to heal the body through sex, then it didn't make sense to deplete the body of all that essential nourishment, it was even better if you could reabsorb it. This was not essential but it helped.

My Advice

The idea of using sexual positions to heal chronic illnesses was written about in ancient Indian medical texts dating to between the tenth and sixth centuries BCE and gradually spread east and west to China, Afghanistan and Persia.

Over time, the knowledge of therapeutic sexual positions has gradually disappeared from popular practice in India. The *Kama Sutra*, for instance, does not categorize positions for healing purposes specifically. It addresses the whole subject in a more general manner, referring to the importance of sexual activity as an essential pillar of life and how it benefits the body, the soul and the mind but not what part of the body it will precisely impact, or how.

Over the centuries many of the ancient texts and manuscripts have been either partially or entirely lost, so how much is missing from the instructions of these positions we cannot be sure of. Our knowledge is incomplete—does it really work, is it only useful for the man or is there any benefit for women as well, if you do it incorrectly can you harm yourself instead, etc?

I would recommend trying it with whatever instructions are available, because you never know how much benefit— mental or physical—you will gain from it. And as far as I can tell there are no reported cases of any negative side effects.

The detailed knowledge and practice of therapeutic sex still exists in China within the Taoist traditions. It is part of an extraordinarily complex philosophy that could take time to assimilate—definitely not for the casual weekender—but it is there.

And finally there is the twenty-first century Western version of therapeutic sex based on scientific research, according to which sex can prevent heart disease, relieve stress and even keep the flu at bay. The instructions seem easier to understand, minus all the complex philosophy, but be warned—when you look under the surface it still comes with its own set of quite stringent rules.

For instance, medicine says having more sex (at least twice a week) raises homocysteine levels and can prevent blood clots and heart attacks—and there are no specific types of positions or thrusts prescribed. The small print, however, is that these

Seema Anand

research findings only apply to men. Extra sex does not create a difference in the homocysteine levels for women at all.

Orgasms have been shown to improve the quality of sleep, thereby relieving stress. The problem however is that most men will have an orgasm between three to fifteen minutes after they begin sex, while most women cannot come to orgasm before at least fifteen to twenty minutes and generally will miss out on it altogether. So it could be a great remedy but depends on who is having the orgasm.

Having regular sex can keep the flu away. The antigens from your lover's saliva will help boost your immune system. The downside—research shows that more sexually active people are exposed to more infections and therefore good hygiene is not just essential, it has to be your religion.

But still—the benefits far outweigh the tedium of the rules.

Sex can help improve brain function—sexual activity grows the nervous tissues around the brain that lead to improved memory and better comprehension. It can make you look younger, it can make you feel happier and more stable.

The only real proviso is—the sex has to be 'good, loving' sex.

Gems and Precious Stones

According to myth, when the gods and the demons joined forces to churn the cosmic ocean to try and get to the nectar of immortality which was sitting right at the bottom, many other strange and wonderful things were thrown out of the waters—among them precious gems and sparkling jewels. They were beautiful and the gods wanted to keep them, but according to the prearranged terms of the churning agreement the jewels were the property of the demons who had gleefully grabbed the gems and stored them in the cavities of their rotting teeth for safekeeping. But soon it was noticed that there was more to the gems than their beauty because no matter how hard the demons worked, they never seemed to get tired—on the contrary, they seemed more rejuvenated with each passing day. It would take a long, long time before the ownership of the jewels finally passed from the demons to the gods. But the gods did not rest until they had them.

Precious stones come from mines deep in the earth or from under the oceans, they are made of the same minerals and substances that nourish the centre of the earth—the core of all life—so they are believed to possess all the secrets of life and regeneration. Gemmology, or the study of gems, is listed as one of the sixty-four skills in the *Kama Sutra*. The understanding of precious stones, their distinguishing features, a detailed knowledge of their uses in medicine, astrology, and Ayurveda, their importance in defining social status, etc. was an essential skill for both the lover and the householder.

Gemstones were also supposed to have great health benefits and Ayurveda dedicates a whole study to the their medicinal power—especially in the use of sexual health. Are you suffering from sexual fatigue? Is age slowing you and your libido down? Been with your partner too long and boredom and monotony has set in? Or is it hormones and mucus discharges? The ancients felt that the answers to all of these problems lay in the use of gems and crystals.

Reduced blood flow to the penis could be corrected with red coral. Diamonds could help a low sex drive. General sexual ineffectiveness can be helped with topaz or any orange-coloured crystal.

Low sex drive? Try garnet or lapis lazuli.

For weak erections, amazonite is recommended.

Premature ejaculation—amber or blue moonstone.

Loss of semen in urine—pearls.

Sexual depression—dark opal.

Gems and stones work on a 'cause and effect' basis—if you are having trouble getting an erection it could be because the blood flow in the lower abdomen is insufficient, the blood flow could be insufficient because the energy is blocked, the energy could be blocked because the kidneys are sluggish and the kidneys could be sluggish because of a problem in the lungs. The ancient Chinese believed that each organ has a mother and father organ that supports its functions—if the kidneys are sluggish they will be nurtured by the lungs which is its mother organ and if they are overactive they will be disciplined by the father organ which is the spleen. So the gems would be used to nourish the parent organ which could then balance the energy in the relevant location in the body.

Gems could be used in several different forms. They could be made into jewellery or talismans but for sexual issues the best method was to ingest them—ground to fine powder and drunk mixed with honey or milk, some were even offered in paan. With gems that could not be ground, like diamonds, it was best to burn them with pure ghee and drink the soot or apply it as an ointment.

In ancient India nine 'basic' gems are mentioned. Each gem is associated with a planet as well as a day of the week and ideally should be used in conjunction with one's individual planetary ruling.

Ruby (Day—Sunday, Planet—Sun)

Powdered and mixed in ghee or honey for best results. Ideal time for ingesting or wearing is on Sundays between 5 and 6 a.m. This is the time when the body's natural sexual energy is at its peak.

The effectiveness of the ruby lies in its red colour—the colour of passion. Because the red colour stems from the heart of the gem, it is not just a surface pigment, it can transfuse its properties into the bloodstream, literally turning the person more 'red blooded'. It is extremely effective in dealing with skin problems like eczema, acne, pimples and sallow complexions; transforming the skin with a youthful red glow, not only to make you happier but calculated to raise the temperature of your partner as well. It is a great remedy for vaginal itches—the friction of sex can sometimes scratch the vulva which in turn causes itching. Rubies were a preventative as well as a treatment for this. But the most popular function of the ruby is its role as the 'kisser's companion'. One doesn't just say 'ruby lips' because of the colour—it was believed that a regular diet of rubies strengthened the gums, which in turn cures bad breath, making your mouth perfect for kissing.

Pearl (Day—Monday, Planet—Moon)

Pearls should be ground by hand using a pestle and mortar and drunk mixed with rose water or other aromatic plant juices, ideally between 5 and 6 a.m.

Pearls are the gem of the moon and like their planetary father, they are the gem of romance. These beautiful beads work in a strange way—they cause excitement by calming. Tension causes irregular breathing which obstructs the blood flow to the genitals, making it more difficult for arousal to take place. If the breathing is calmed, the blood will flow better, the blockages are removed and it improves erection and clitoral engorgement.

Pearls are used for breathing-related problems—they settle and regulate the breath which has the effect of reducing anxiety. This further calms the heart, allowing other channels to open up and energy to flow to other parts of the body.

The changing phases of the moon shift the erogenous zones from one part of the body to the other—pearls allow the sensations in each erogenous zone to intensify.

According to ancient texts, the oyster shell that houses the pearl can also be crushed and drunk to help in improving your sexual performance. The oyster is a prime example of sexual self-sufficiency—it can become both male or female at will. Through the course of its life an oyster changes its gender numerous times. And so the shell is believed to carry incredible sexual power.

Even ordinary shells can be used although they are much, much weaker.

Coral (Day—Tuesday, Planet—Mars)

They should be crushed and taken with boiled milk, ideally between 11 a.m. and 1 p.m. on Tuesdays. Corals can also be worn as rings very effectively. If you are collecting the soot of corals, the cup should be made of brass.

Corals are known for bringing harmony back to a marriage by fixing the problems that arise from boredom, monotony and age in long-term relationships. Corals will regulate blood flow in the genital and abdominal regions of the body which builds up sexual energy—allowing men to hold their erections for longer and women to have more natural lubrication. This will bring back a renewed interest in sex. If applied as an ointment to the stomach of a pregnant woman it can prevent miscarriages.

Emerald (Day—Wednesday, Planet—Mercury)

Crushed and mixed in raw milk, to be had between 5 and 7 a.m.

Emeralds improve blood circulation, increase virility and destroy the toxins in the body that can be an obstacle to potency. But the emerald has even greater powers in helping sexual health than the merely physical. The mineral composition of this gem is such that it energizes the mind so that you can effectively fight negativity within yourself and help you to become more understanding towards your partner.

Emeralds should be used under strict guidance because in sexual matters they suit very few people.

Topaz (Day—Thursday, Planet—Jupiter)

Crush and drink with honey, ideal time between 5 and 7 a.m.

According to myth, topaz is the 'breath of intercourse', Kamadeva wore a topaz on his belt buckle to make sure that his potency never decreased.

If worn on the left arm, some believed a topaz amulet could protect the wearer from dark magic and the greed of others. In addition, this could relieve arthritic pain, improve digestion, help in weight loss and attract love. If taken in a potion, some believed it could cure an even wider range of ailments.

The topaz comes in different colours. Each one has its uses.

Sapphire (Day—Friday, Planet—Saturn)

Crushed in milk and drunk between 5 and 7 a.m.

Blue sapphires are a dangerous gem. They belong to the god Shani and like their master they have a reputation for being malicious, so watch out when using this stone. But for those of you who are friends with this gem, sapphires are the stones for all things erotic. And so potent was their effect that according to ancient sources sapphires were also crushed and served in paan during the course of seduction. They destroy all toxins, including poisonous thoughts.

Diamond (Day—Saturday, Planet—Venus)

Diamonds are too hard to be ground into a powder so their soot is used. Burn in a pure silver container with ghee to collect the soot and drink mixed with honey. If worn as jewellery, diamonds should be worn on the finger or the upper arm. Ideal time is between 5 and 7 a.m. on Saturdays.

Different types of diamonds are to be worn by men and by women.

The diamond is the favourite gem for Ayurveda practitioners. It is called the healer of healers because your condition can be treated simply by being in the vicinity of its brilliance. Diamonds can be used as general medicine for all symptoms of declining sexual health—it is a fix-all. It was also considered one of the best treatments for age-related impotence.

But here's the catch—it has to be the right kind of diamond. It is the most complicated of gems and the qualities, peculiarities and traits of a diamond are so varied that the combinations of what you can or can't wear are open to hundreds of interpretations.

Diamonds are categorized by colour—Brahman (white), Kshatriya (red), Vaishya (yellow) and Sudra (black). They are categorized by gender—male, female and neuter. Brilliant, flawless, round stones with a large surface are male diamonds, round but with some flaws are female, triangles or rectangles with flaws are neuter. There is no universally acknowledged table of flaws because what counts as a flaw in one category is not a flaw in another. Each kind of diamond has a different presiding deity—a hexagonal white diamond is Indra (the king of gods), a black one in the shape of a snake's head is Yamaraj (the god of death), a diamond with a blood red spot in the middle is for the power of Kali and one in which the dot is turned slightly to the left is for all the Mahavidyas (the tantric goddesses of supreme knowledge).

You have to pick the one that is specific for you otherwise it will not have the effect you want. Unlike the Western idea of 'diamonds are a girl's best friend', Eastern philosophy says if the combination is wrong it can be your worst enemy.

Crystals

According to mythology, when the demon Vala was murdered and dismembered by the gods, his semen spilled onto the earth and became crystals. Crystals are good for all aspects of your sex life, and are especially beneficial for hormones.

Crystals are known as 'catalysts' because you can mix the crystal with almost anything and it will enhance the power of the other substance as well. There are many types of crystals and each one has its own function but the best are the colourless ones because they most closely contain the properties of Vala's semen. Crystals are not as concentrated as some of the other gems so they need to be used over a longer period of time to be truly effective. But by the same token, they are also not dangerous and do not have any negative effects.

Hessonite and cat's eyes are respectively Rahu and Ketu, the North and South nodes of the moon. They are best mixed in honey and ingested between 5 and 7 a.m.

The story of these two gems as well as of their planetary masters is steeped in violence. Rahu and Ketu are the two halves of a demon who tried to drink the forbidden nectar of immortality and was punished by being chopped into two. He is destined to live in eternal dismemberment. Cat's eyes were created from the shrieks of terror of another dismemberment (that of the demon Vala) and hessonite came from his fingernails as they were ripped out and thrown into the ocean.

Despite the violence associated with their origins, crystals are unusually benevolent.

They are said to safeguard you from scandal and from losing your reputation. And cat's eyes are also good for healing anal fissures and treating vaginal discharges.

These are just a handful of the gems and stones that our

ancient texts have written about and, regardless of their purity or value or rarity, each one has its own power that you can tap into.

My Advice

When the *Kama Sutra* speaks of gemmology as one of the sixty-four essential skills, it is not quite as simple as knowing the names of precious stones or when to wear them or what kind you can afford to buy.

The efficacy of gems depends on their purity, but after all what is purity? All gems are mined from under the ground or found in water and they take on the properties of the elements that they come in contact with. So things like dust, dents, scratch lines, etc. may come from the earth while the glossiness and smoothness may be because the stone has been sitting in moving water for a very long time—so if you are more in need of the earth element then the 'impurities' are better for you.

Most gems are minerals, but some, like pearls and corals, for instance, are of animal origin and have a different molecular make-up.

To understand the benefits of gems and how to use each one for the correct circumstances meant having a pretty good understanding of mineralogy, zoology, botany and geology.

For instance, did you know that rubies are picked for their weight while diamonds are best picked for their lightness—the most expensive diamonds should be able to float on water.

With the emerald, hold it on the palm of your hand and face the sun. If the gem is genuine, its light will reflect towards you.

Place a sapphire in a bowl of milk—the milk should take on a bluish tinge from the lustre of the gem.

Hold a ruby between the thumb and forefinger—if the

light reflects upwards it is a brilliant quality gem, a downward reflection means medium quality and sideways is inferior.

When a cat's eye is placed on a mirror, the reflection shows a series of plumb lines forming around it—two or three lines mean it is a brilliant stone, five or six lines for a medium stone, broken lines denote a poor quality stone.

But most importantly one must be sensible about gems.

The ancients may have believed that ingesting a gem was very effective in treating ailments but we now know better. Under no circumstances should you try and ingest them. No one knows what quality of gemstone you have, what its mineral composition is and what it is likely to do to you.

Wear them, enjoy them, be seduced by them—in good health.

Shringhar

Kamadeva had set out to distract Shiva, to break his meditation and turn his thoughts towards love. Kama had asked all his companions to go with him—Vasant (spring), Megha (the heavily laden rain clouds that epitomize romance and desire, irresistible to all lovers), Sugandha (the perfumed breeze), the Gandharvas (the heavenly musicians) and others.

Truth be told Kamadeva was petrified—he was setting out to wilfully destroy Shiva's meditation and Shiva was not known for his understanding nature or sweetness of temperament. The great god had warned everyone that he did not want to be approached and no one else had dared go against his will—not even Vishnu.

But then again the God of Love was also a little bit arrogant. After all, he had never failed before, no one had ever been able to resist his magic till now.

And he was right. He had, in the end, succeeded in breaking Shiva's meditation but he had paid for it with his life. Furious at being disturbed, the great god had turned the cosmic rage of his third eye on him and Kamadeva had disintegrated into a little heap of ash right where he stood.

But what of all his companions—springtime, rain clouds, scented breeze, the bees, parrots, fish—who had gone with him? They had all made a run for it, trying desperately to hide themselves where Shiva's fire could not hurt them. And what better place than in the delightful and charming personae of women everywhere.

The bees that made up the string of Kamadeva's bow camouflaged themselves as the curly black lustrous hair of a woman. The lotus shoots that had once formed the bow found their hiding place in her slim, tender arms. The luminous full moon merged into her face and her two eyes became the hiding place for the fish that are Kamadeva's victory banner. The 'sandalwood-scented breeze'—Kamadeva's most irresistible companion—could be found in her breath while the red spring flowers nestled into her lower lip. His victory conch (that beautiful, slender, long, ivory-coloured shell) headed for her neck while his earthenware pots disguised themselves as her full breasts and the wheels of his chariot as her ample buttocks.

Her beautiful, swirling navel welcomed the half-opened lotus bud that Kamadeva wore behind his ear, her two thighs, robust and plump, housed the Love God's victory pillars which were made from the trunks of the banana tree, the moonbeams settled into her fingers, the thousand-petalled lotus blossomed into her feet and so on, till everything had found a hiding place.

So Kamadeva was dead but all of his tools of seduction and romance were alive and functioning, and they had taken on a physical form as well—they were the manifestations of Shringhar Rasa.

But here the story twists again.

A heartbroken Rati (Kamadeva's wife) decides to kill herself. With him gone, there is no reason for her to continue living. The gods, however, strike a deal with her. They will eventually restore him to life and return him to her—love, seduction, desire cannot be killed off—how will the world survive without him? But meanwhile she must agree to continue his work. It will be her duty to regulate spring and the southern sandalwood scented breezes, to manage the fragrance of the flowers and the mystique of the moon, to lead that whole army of bees and parrots and fish and flowers so that they can continue to raise desire, so that ascetics can continue to break their oaths of celibacy, so that lovers can continue to rule supreme.

Rati agreed. She took over the armies of love and desire, the seasons and reasons of sensuality, the techniques and arts of seduction, all the living symbols of her beloved husband's work. And she set about creating the manuals of love.

They say that Rati created the Solah Shringhar. Solah means sixteen and the word 'shringhar' means ornamentation.

Her first job was to organize the rank and file of Kamadeva's companions who were now hiding in every woman. Each aspect of the woman was already a living symbol of seduction, a little facet of the magic of the love god, shringhar was simply Rati's way of teaching women how to enhance and animate each of these aspects to create the right mood.

Rati's shringhar was more than just make-up—it was how the woman brought alive her beauty, it was how she expressed her feelings and what emotions she aroused in her lover. Each adornment had a reason.

Lips

The lips are the first doorway to pleasure, holding all the secrets of heaven, like two parallel waves of the river of delight that meet at the corners of the mouth to create whirlpools of such mysterious depths that a lover could not help but drown in them.

The upper lip was the bow of Kamadeva and the lower lip was the hiding place of the red bandhuk flowers. The bandhuk is a bright red flower that blossoms at midday and, unlike other flowers, it stays open all night, closing early the following morning—much as the lips of the beloved which blossom all night under the touch of the lover.

The gently undulating upper lip was the symbol of modesty while the full red lower lip was the image of sensuality and sexuality.

The embrace on the upper lip was of a private nature— which means that you did not leave tooth marks or swellings on the upper lip while kissing. The lower lip, on the other hand, was to be adorned with bite marks—red and slightly swollen. A lower lip was the public expression of your passion and a lip that didn't carry the marks of passion was unadorned and lacking in beauty. The very centre of the lower lip was repeatedly bitten with the tooth to create a little indentation, it was a mark of a highly passionate nature and an essential ornament. Lips were coloured red with the help of paan and vermilion which were then rubbed with wax to make sure the colour didn't come off.

The 'whirlpools' or dimples at the corners of the mouth were also essential adornments and were enhanced with small moles, especially on the left corner of the mouth. A kiss had to begin at the left corner of the mouth and come to the centre.

Scented breath

Next was the scented breath of the nayika (the beautiful woman), where the perfumed spring breezes had camouflaged themselves—they became the 'lovelorn sigh'. A frequently recurring theme in medieval poetry is the nayika sighing, and so exquisitely fragrant is her breath that flowers blossom out of season, throwing the birds and bees into confusion—is it spring already? As tools of seduction go, the sigh was one of the most important adornments of the woman—when done right it made her lips pout and her breasts rise and fall, her neck curved sideways to show off the delicate profile and the shoulder bones, her waist arched upwards and her eyes took on a dreamy faraway look. In miniature painting it was depicted as the woman stretching her linked hands over her head.

The *Kama Sutra* says sighs could be 'soundless' or 'with sound', like a moan. But the most important thing with the sigh was that it had to be expelled on a fluttery breath through the indentation in the centre of the lower lip, making the cleft quiver just a little—that little flutter was meant to be the most erotic of symbols.

Fragrant breath was a very big deal. There was an inordinate amount of attention paid to the perfuming of the mouth. Tender mango shoots, camphor and cloves were eaten to sweeten the breath. The mouth was freshened with betel and brushed with twigs that had been soaked in sweet-smelling mixtures. Drinking water was scented and men would even keep perfumed concoctions near the bed to combat foul smells that can build up in the woman's mouth at night.

Fragrancing the mouth was done in honour of the goddess of speech—the ability to play with words made you more desirable.

Eyes

The fish from Kamadeva's victory banner had fled to the eyes of the beauty.

In paintings and poetry, the eyes of the nayika are always described as fish-shaped, starting at the nose and extending all the way to the hairline where they end in a sharp point. The eyes were shaped with kohl but, according to Rati, their real adornment was the sidelong glances that were thrown from the corners of the eyes. There was a whole vocabulary of glances that the eyes had to be able to convey—a very detailed vocabulary.

Rati says that the eyes must be as proficient as a dance teacher if they are to make the lover dance to their tune.

Eyebrows

Two of the five arrows of Kamadeva sought refuge in the beauty's eyebrows.

The eyebrows are said to be the cooling spirits of dawn and dusk descended to frame the burning glances of the beautiful woman. Like the eyes, the brows too have a language of their own but it is a language most feared by lovers because unlike the eyes the eyebrows are warriors—two arched eyebrows indicate disbelief, one arched brow for sarcasm, meeting together in the middle for anger.

The eyebrows were ornamented with tamala leaves cut out in different shapes—often pairs of birds or other animals, so that when placed together they looked as though they were embracing. Cutting shapes was one of the sixty-four skills of the *Kama Sutra*.

Breasts

The beautiful rounded breasts of the nayika are the earthenware pots of Kamadeva—full, heavy and golden, like the baked earth from which they were made. They are adorned with colours, designs and perfumes to enhance their beauty.

When we talk of tattooing and body art in Solah Shringhar we generally assume it means henna patterns on the hands and the feet. But in the time of the *Kama Sutra* it was literally body art—designs and patterns painted on different parts of the body (breasts, cheeks and forehead) in order to enhance them.

The painting and colouring of breasts was a fine art and had their own code. On moonlit nights they were coloured with white sandalwood paste which reflected the pale glow of the moonlight and made them appear fairer. On darker nights they were rubbed with a saffron and oil mixture to create a reddish glow. There were different pigments for daytime, for summer, for winter etc.

Over this were placed 'makarika' patterns (specific types of fernlike leaves and flowers) which were painted on with black agaru paste (a highly fragrant sort of aloe) using the forefinger.

> In private the girlfriend pretended to draw upon her breasts
> The usual design
> But drew instead
> The quivering hand of her lover...
> —Bhanu Datta

It was inauspicious for a woman to be without breast paintings. In *Kadambri* we see King Tarapeed telling Queen Vilasavati off for not being adorned with agaru paintings on her breasts—he tells her it is an ill omen.

Teeth

Two of Kamadeva's arrows had made a beeline for the beauty's teeth—one arrow was of pure white jasmine flowers and the other of deep crimson Ashoka flowers. The jasmine flowers became small white teeth like little pearls in row.

But why the arrow of red flowers for the teeth?

In the time of the *Kama Sutra* coloured teeth were considered ornamental. As I've mentioned earlier, the fashion of colouring the teeth went out of mode by the sixth century. Instead, it became de rigueur to colour the gums black, in order to better show the delicate white of the teeth, a trend that persisted well into the eighteenth century.

The real beauty of the teeth was seen through the kind of love bite you left—that would show not only whether the shape and size etc. were good but also what you could do with them.

Hair

Kamadeva had been standing poised, ready to shoot his flower arrow at Shiva, the string of his sugarcane and lotus shoot bow pulled back tight all the way to the corner of his right eye when Shiva had opened his third eye. Kama was incinerated where he stood. The bees that make up the string of Kamadeva's bow had been closest to his face as he went up in smoke—they had barely managed to escape the force of that universe-destroying fire. They had scattered everywhere in panic but very quickly gathered again in a swarm and settled into the hair of women.

Hair was supposed to be curly, black, vigorously healthy, perfumed at all times; it was the crowning glory, the chief ornament of a woman's seductive powers—the shringhar of shringhar!

The skill was in knowing how to dress it for what occasion.

Neatly tied with flowers and jewels—you were at a respectable occasion.

One strand escaping onto the forehead in public—you were letting your lover see how much you missed him.

Dishevelled hair across the pillow—you had just finished making love.

The flowers from your hair lying on the ground—you had been on top during the lovemaking.

Styling and dressing hair was one of the sixty-four skills of the *Kama Sutra*. Different hairstyles held different messages.

The shifting phases of the moon impact the erogenous zones of the body—with each phase a different point becomes more sensitive. On the night of the full moon it is the head and the hair which is the most excitable and shampooing and combing the beloved's hair was used as foreplay on that night.

Perfume

With all her freshly blooming flowers nestled into the hidden and unhidden parts of the body as many different scents, Vasant (Spring) is a favourite companion of Kamadeva.

Each part of the body had to be perfumed with different fragrances because each perfume had its own impact on the senses. Different perfumes were worn according to day or night, season, occasion, age etc. Some were cooling, some produced heat, some calmed you while other inflamed your senses, there were more variations than you can begin to imagine.

Perfume was the single most important ornamentation for the body and in the third century it seems to have been such big business that even the *Arthashastra* devotes an entire chapter to the subject. Kautilya, as I've mentioned earlier, tells us that perfumed resins were hoarded in royal treasuries like precious gems.

Feet

The thousand-petalled lotus blossomed into the foot.

Feet have a very special place in the seduction of the senses. Watching a woman's foot in dance, its strength and mobility, its ability to raise or drop your heart rate just by changing the tempo was erotically charged. Feet were magic. A well-trained foot could delight and seduce in ways that no other part of the body could.

The underside of the foot was painted with red lac. It highlighted the arches and the deep crimson contrasted with the skin to make the foot appear a more delicate colour. The alta paste left footprints in the wake of the beauty as she walked—a conceit that has been the delight of poets over the centuries.

The delicate foot, perfectly reddened at the arches, glittering with toe rings, jewelled at the ankle, supporting the shapely calf was like the living staff of Kamadeva—casting spells of enchantment.

But the foot itself was also an ornament of love—it was the shringhar of the man's head. As we have seen, the beloved's foot on her lover's head denoted that they had just made love. One of the most popular sexual positions would have placed her foot on his head leaving behind the streaks of the alta as a telltale red mark of their actions.

An entire genre of literature was created to sing of the erotic possibilities of delicate feet placed on the man's head. The foot of the nayika was adored for what it could do—that's what made it worthy of worship.

Ankle

The ankle was where the root of the thousand-petalled lotus had hidden itself. Rati declared that the erotic appeal of the foot would stem from the ankle. It was the ankle that rested on the lover's shoulders during sex, it was the ankle that carried the jingling anklets that measured the tempo of the lovemaking, it was the ankle that gave the foot the flexibility to turn this way and that in order to seduce.

The tapering ankle was the sartaj (the crowning glory) of the leg and the ornament of the ankle was the well-trained foot.

Neck

The victory conch of Kamadeva, exquisitely wrought, was fashioned by the waves of the ocean as they tenderly moulded it, turning it first this way, then that, till they were finally satisfied with the result. It had taken centuries to create. Kamadeva had put it to his lips every day. That conch had found a home in the neck of the beauty—so that it could always be at the lips of the lover!

The long, slender neck is the most seductive part of the woman's body and a very potent erogenous zone. Kisses placed on the neck are the most effective. As we have seen, the best recommended shringhar for the neck is the necklace of love bites known as the 'Dot' or 'Bindu'.

The seduction of the neck lay in the way it moved— throw it back a bit and the chin is raised in defiance, bend it forward and the nayika is the image of modesty, incline it to one side—she is the epitome of sarcasm, turn it to one side and there is a tantrum.

The neck was dusted with sandalwood powder to give it a whiter appearance and was generally perfumed with jasmine. Jasmine was the scent of innocence and was supposed to put the lover at ease.

Hands

Home of the trembling moonbeams, the hands are as fragile as moonlight, the fingers are tremulous as they impatiently twist and tug at the strands of hair coming loose from her braid, the palms hold the nectar of love and desire for the lover to drink from.

The feather-light touch of the fingers as they played across the lover's body, the firm command of the pad of the thumb as it rubbed his lower lip, casting the invisible yet irresistible snare made up of moonbeams—that was the legacy of Kamadeva's companion to the hands. Rati added that the ornamentation of a woman's hands should be her deftness and skill as she performs any task.

As opposed to the full hand of henna which is now in fashion, at that time just the inside tips of the fingers were coloured in order to highlight the pale flesh of the palm. On the thumb the nayika wore an 'arsi' which was a large ring with a mirror in the middle. The back of the hand was rubbed with sandalwood or other pigments and fragrances and makarika designs using black aloe paste would be painted on it.

As with the others, the real shringhar of the hands was in what they could do. So, in the time of the *Kama Sutra*, daily ornamentation was kept to a minimum.

Navel

The half-opened lotus bud which was the ear ornament of the god of love hid in the navel of the nayika. The lotus bud was the timekeeper of the lovers—the lotus bud bloomed when the sun came up letting you know that day had begun and lovemaking was at an end. Like the navel, it was the dividing line between the attainable and the intimate. The lower garment was tied just below the navel and only the lover was permitted to touch it.

The navel of the beloved, both hidden and revealed at the same time, carries an unparalleled fascination, like a mysterious eddy with unknown depths. You know you could drown but you cannot help yourself either. It held the promise of excitement, of intimacy.

The navel was covered with jewelled belts and sashes—rubies and gold were considered the most beneficial material to wear on this part of the body. These belts too were made in such a fashion that they held the potential of movement—they covered the navel but always looked like they would move at any moment from their spot and reveal that vortex of ecstasy.

The navel was scented with very heady musk—it's a small area so the perfume had to be strong enough to draw you in. One of the major erotic arteries runs through the navel, which makes it a very sensitive and exciting point of stimulation.

Ear

The pink ocean lotuses took refuge in the ears.

Legend has it that pink ocean lotuses never wilt. The Sea God created them to adorn the corridors of his underwater palace, but when the lotuses realized how dark and deserted his palace was, they abandoned him to look for places more worthy of their beauty. They had become part of Kamadeva's train and after his death they took up residence in the ears of women.

The ear was always visible in public (hair was worn tied back) and was regularly ornamented with earrings of different shapes and sizes. The lobes were pinched to make them red and slightly swollen—it was a mark of beauty.

The true beauty of the ear was to be able to understand the subtleties of musical compositions.

Buttocks

At the burning up of Kamadeva, the wheels of his chariot fled to hide in the women's buttocks.

'She of the beautiful bottom' is a title constantly used in the *Kama Sutra*. Beautifully rounded buttocks were the mark of ultimate beauty, the firm fullness accentuated further by the curve of the beloved's narrow waist. Women cultivated a swaying walk, 'gajgamini', heavy and sultry like the undulating of an elephant. It was the ultimate in seduction.

One of the large erotic nerves runs through the buttocks and, according to the *Kama Sutra*, this artery needs a lot work— one must dig in hard with the nails in order to stimulate it. The nail marks left as a result are the shringhar of the buttocks.

Looping necklaces of scratches are made on the buttocks, the hips and the upper thighs and each time the beloved sees the scratches her love is revived. If another man chances to see these marks—even if he is of firm and pure character—he will find himself attracted to 'her of the beautiful bottom'.

Garlands and girdles

Kamadeva's army of flowers made up the girdles and garlands worn by the nayika.

They were so important to the everyday life of the women that Rati includes this in her list of shringhar.

Girdles and garlands were made up of different flowers depending on circumstances, seasons, physiology etc.

Garlands were worn around the neck, primarily to fight

off any unwanted sweaty odours but for other reasons too. For instance, a woman going out to meet her lover on a rainy night would wear garlands of kadamba flowers, which bloom in the monsoon. Or, as we have seen, a garland of amaranth flowers was worn for lovemaking because the petals are tough and would not easily shed during embraces.

Girdles were worn around the hips and were important pieces of jewellery. The hips were massaged with oils and perfume mixed with turmeric before the girdle was placed on the hip bone, just below the navel. Girdles were supposed to measure the sway of the hips as the woman walked. If the hips didn't sway far enough the girdle would slip off.

Here, the older woman with her fuller hips for once had the advantage over her younger rival.

My Advice

The Solah Shringhar has changed many times over the centuries. Fashions have changed, staining the teeth red and black died out as far back as the fourth century and a woman no longer goes out of her way to develop large buttocks that resemble the wheels of a chariot nor does she pinch her earlobes to make them swell up as a mark of beauty.

The recurring motif in Rati's shringhar is mobility. Seduction lies in movement—in lightness and freedom—what you do and how you do it.

Today's idea of shringhar, however, is often such a heavily made-up and bejewelled look that it constricts movement and can feel rather oppressive.

If I had to translate Rati's advice to our times I have one word for it—exercise!

The beauty of a strong, mobile body surpasses everything—

fit and glowing with good health. Because that is the body that can find the energy to make love and to enjoy it to the fullest. Rati's shringhar speaks to our individual selves, it gives the essence rather than the instruction.

Shringhar is auspicious and whichever ornament you choose to adorn yourself with should feel good.

The Courtesan Fantasy—
Jewellery and the Arts of Seduction

There's something about jewellery that can change an ordinary act of sex into something far more romantic and elegant and gorgeous. It adds a sense of anticipation. You can almost see yourself seated on silk sheets, a glossy mass of hair tumbling down your shoulders, the picture of sensuality, while your partner sits at your feet looking at you with awe and desire because you are the mistress of seduction, you are the goddess of the sixty-four skills of the *Kama Sutra*, you are the brightness that is going to light up his night.

And all this is possible just by putting on some jewellery? According to the *Kama Sutra*—yes!

If you look at the erotic paintings and sculptures of ancient India you will notice that the people are often naked but always wearing a lot of jewellery.

The *Kama Sutra* says each piece of jewellery carries its own meaning, its own significance and each one denotes a different position.

Jewellery was divided into jingling ornaments, quiet ornaments and 'other' ornaments.

'Loud' (jingling or flashy) jewellery was worn for specific purposes—for instance, by a woman who wanted to attract the attention of a particular man, or to denote her position as a mistress. Wives and women of the upper classes wore more subtle jewellery—they were not to attract attention to themselves. Superior courtesans who were attached to just one patron also generally wore quiet jewellery unless they wished to indicate that they would be performing certain positions in which case they could wear certain ornaments specific to their needs. Regular courtesans and normal prostitutes wore jingly jewellery. A wife could wear loud jewellery to please her husband in private.

'Other' ornaments were worn if the woman was sneaking out to meet a clandestine lover. Then she would not wear loud jewellery—she would not want to draw attention to herself and she would not wear her marital jewellery because she wouldn't want to be recognized.

The girdle of bells around the waist

As I've mentioned, at the time of the *Kama Sutra*, it was believed that women weren't supposed to be on top during lovemaking. Being on top was indicative of power and choice, according to the ancient Indian texts it was 'very hard work'—either way, it was not the natural position for women. But, the *Kama Sutra* says, a woman could be on top if she was very good at lovemaking. And to be very good meant she had to be able to bring herself and her lover to orgasm by the movement of her hips—not her torso, just the hips. To prove their prowess, the really accomplished courtesans would wear a girdle of jingling ghungroos around the waist during sex and make sure none of them made a sound. Thus, the girdle became a metaphor in ancient Sanskrit literature to suggest this position. If the author mentioned that 'the beautiful woman had put on her girdle' you knew she had taken her position on top. Or if the man sent the girdle to his mistress as a gift, she knew what he was expecting that day. Eventually, it became the mark of a supremely gifted lover. If at a social occasion the women invited to entertain dignitaries wore these girdles then you knew that the guests were extremely important and of high status.

Jingling anklets

There is a position called 'splitting the bamboo' where the woman lies on her back and alternately places her feet, one at a time, on the man's shoulders. First, the left foot is placed on the corresponding shoulder, then taken down. After that, the right foot is placed on the corresponding shoulder before being taken down. And she continues to do this all the way through the entire lovemaking, in rhythm with his thrusts. And she wears her jingliest anklets for this—to show that she can keep pace with his rhythm no matter how fast he goes.

The nine-stringed pearl necklace

This necklace is worn for lovemaking in the sitting position. As I've mentioned, furniture was very different when the *Kama Sutra* was written so lovers would be sitting on a mattress on the floor, propped up against cushions. In this position, the woman sits on the man's lap, feet around his hips, upper body bent back, leaning on her hands. The necklace with nine strings would have been like a moving screen, every now and then allowing glimpses of well-oiled breasts rubbed with sandalwood paste, covered with beads of sweat.

Earrings

Long earrings or 'kundal' were worn while on top or in sitting positions—the swinging and grazing of earrings against a cheek glowing with perspiration during the exertions of sex were the ultimate in poetic beauty. Short earrings or 'darshan' were worn when lying down. In the epic *Amarushataka*, the thoroughly embarrassed young bride is seen stuffing her ruby 'kundal' into the parrot's mouth when, in the presence of the elders, the bird is repeating what the young couple had done at night. And from that lovely little gesture even we know what she had done.

Diamond or pearl clips worn in the hair

Poets have waxed lyrical about the mass of a woman's loosened hair, like dark storm clouds around the face of the moon, tumbling over her shoulders; of the flowers that were holding up her hair but now lie strewn across the floor. In positions where the woman was on top, or sitting up, she took on the role of thrusting. Her skill lay in making these clips come loose and fall to the floor with her exertions and movements. For the lover the sight of the hair ornaments lying on the floor was as arousing as the act of sex itself and only the very blessed would get to see this—it meant that they had experienced utterly ecstatic lovemaking.

Lower abdomen girdle

Possibly the most romantic piece of jewellery to be had, this was a thin gold chain worn low on the abdomen and strung with rubies, each stone acknowledging her proficiency in the sixty-four arts of the *Kama Sutra*. The rubies were typically anniversary gifts from a besotted and grateful lover. The more respectable version of this was a girdle called the mekhala which was worn on the outside of the clothes and was suitable for wives and other women of the household. The mekhala was made up of several chains that hang in loops from the hips down the thighs—the number of chains represented the social, marital and financial status of the woman. These chains generally did not have beads on them but occasionally could—only a maximum of four per chain. Remember, this was for respectability, wives wore mekhalas too. In the epic poem *Malvikagnimitra*, Queen Iravati (drunk and furious) tries to beat her husband with her mekhala because she suspects him of having been unfaithful—the very piece of jewellery he had given her to tell her how much he appreciated her skill in the sixty-four arts of the *Kama Sutra*.

Men wore jewellery for sex too and of the jewellery worn by men the most special were the garlands of fresh flowers. Different flowers indicated different occasions and intentions. As we have seen, a garland of yellow amaranth flowers was worn for a private rendezvous with the beloved—because these flowers did not crush or shed easily with the weight of embraces.

Over the centuries, people have created their own jewellery traditions.

Legend has it that one of the Mewar maharajas had in his collection a pair of diamond eyebrows, to be hooked over the ears and worn like spectacles, which was worn by his favourite concubine. The 'eyebrows' would be carried by the chief eunuch of the harem to the lucky lady—that was her invitation to the maharajas's bed.

Natwar Singh, in his book *Freedom at Midnight*, writes of Maharaja Bhupinder Singh of Patiala, well known for his sexual excesses, who used to give public audience once a year in nothing but a diamond breastplate and a full and glorious erection—proof of the dimensions of the princely organ (there had been malicious gossip of his diminishing abilities) and, as he believed, his virility radiated magic powers to bring plentiful crops and drive evil spirits from the land.

My Advice

We know that role play can add variety and excitement to any sexual relationship but in practical terms it's not always possible. We all fantasize about sexual role play but for most women it is still an awkward thing to suggest.

Well, here's your answer to role play—jewellery. And I don't mean leather and chains—I am talking about beautiful, dress-up jewellery, the sort of thing you would wear to go out.

Wearing jewellery is a subtle 'dressing up' that doesn't need words.

There is a romance to it that is very easy to tap into.

Have your own special code for what each piece will mean to you. It can suggest a particular memory or date or event.

Leave a piece of jewellery by your partner's bedside as a message for what you plan to do for him that day. Or send her a piece of jewellery to suggest what you are looking forward to. Let the excitement build up all day. It's like making a date for sex but with the promise of an added extra—a favourite position or something unusual.

You could even have something that signifies a challenge—when you receive this it's your turn to think of something new!

The Sixty-Four Skills

The *Kama Sutra* gives a list of sixty-four skills that men and women must master if they are to excel in the arts of seduction. It sets them out in great and diligent detail. Anyone who can master these skills will become a brilliant lover desired by everyone.

A quick glance at the skills, however, can leave you feeling confused. One can understand the purpose behind music or dance but how did knowing how to be skilled at quail or cock fights make you a more desirable lover? Or cutting shapes out of leaves—what does that have to do with anything at all?

The sixty-four skills were meant to develop you as a more rounded person—they included mental, physical and verbal accomplishments because the more interesting and accomplished you were and the more varied your interests, the more attractive that made you. In particular, an enormous amount of attention was paid to 'brain games'—the art of repartee, expertise at riddles, conundrums etc. because intelligence is the sexiest thing of all.

Each of the sixty-four skills had a purpose of its own— some have outlived their relevance, others are essential even today. But even the skills that seem obvious are not quite as basic as we think.

So let's upskill.

1-3—Singing, Playing Musical Instruments and Dancing

Skills one, two and three are singing, playing musical instruments and dancing respectively. We start with these as a tribute to the Gandharvas (celestial musicians) and the Apsaras (celestial nymphs) who are the heavenly patrons of the arts of seduction. According to myth, when Kamadeva was incinerated by Shiva, all of his jobs were allocated to other celestials in order to keep 'love' alive. The Gandharvas and the Apsaras took on the responsibilities of music and dance. They perform in the court of Indra (the king of the heavens) and Indra has decreed that nothing shall exceed the Shringhar Rasa (erotic emotions) that this generates. We as human beings dance and play music to imitate the celestial seducers and their arts.

4—Drawing

Drawing was a very important tool of seduction. Men were taught to draw portraits of the beloved as a technique of foreplay. 'Keep paper and chalk handy and draw her'—it focuses your attention on her, maintains eye contact and makes her feel very desirable.

Men and women painted the walls of the house to enhance and ornament it, particularly the rooms that were used for sex where scenes were painted to create the right mood. The *Kama Sutra* says that different types of women need different environments to really bring their passions to full arousal. For some women, sex was best at the water's edge, for others it was a forest clearing. The water's edge and the forest clearing were brought indoors through painted murals. In the story of Kadambari, when her lover Prince Chandrapala enters the apartment, he thinks he has wandered into the heavenly court of Indra which is hidden amongst the clouds—such realistic murals covered the walls of her bedroom that he became lost in wonder.

Another very popular method of mentally overpowering a recalcitrant lover was to cover the walls with portraits of yourself. When the potential lover entered, even if he or she wanted to keep a strict control over themselves they could not—because everywhere they turned they found themselves looking into the eyes of their seducer.

5—Cutouts made from Leaf, Paper or Peels

Shapes were cut out from leaves, paper or peels to be used as forehead ornaments, as part of the Solah Shringhar. The most commonly used material was leaves. They were also used as shadow puppets. Two birds (or other animals) would be cut out and using their shadows on the wall the lover would tell his beloved love stories, ending with the animals (and lovers) coming together in a kiss. This was part of the entertainment and games that the lover was supposed to provide before sex.

6 and 7—Adorning an Idol with Rice Powder and Flowers

Flower arrangements were used to beautify meeting places and personal apartments to make them more conducive to love games. The idols and temples of the God of Love were decorated with flowers and rangoli to invite blessings.

8—Dyes and Colourants for the Body and Teeth

The body was rubbed with different coloured pastes for different occasions. To go out for a walk or to attend a performance where the lover would be present, the breasts were rubbed with a mixture of saffron and oil to give them a glow—particularly the cleavage. During lovemaking, the breast (or chest) would be rubbed with sandalwood paste which left a slightly whitish mark on the chest of the lover—the ancient Indian equivalent of 'you're mine and don't you forget it'. The soles and sides of the feet were painted with red lac. As mentioned earlier, in the time of the *Kama Sutra*, colouring the teeth—red from red lac or black from black aloe paste or tobacco—was an ornamental art (shringhar) which all lovers would have practiced. Good quality teeth, the kind that you could give love bites with, would have a smooth shiny surface that could easily absorb colour.

9 and 10—Decorating Floors and Bed Arrangements

The floor was decorated with mosaics of emeralds, chips or other stones. Low 'beds' would be placed in the middle of the room and covered with arrangements and people would sit on these for eating their meals. So it was more like the modern-day equivalent of laying a beautiful dining table where you entertained your lover.

11 and 12—Playing Musical Bowls filled with Water and Water Squirting Games

Water-filled glasses have the ability to produce notes at 4,000 hertz, which is often beyond the range of the human ear, but one feels the vibrations resonating and so one can feel the impact of the music (rasa). Because of this, it was believed to have magical properties to arouse passions and so was extremely important as a seduction aid.

Water squirting games are associated with the Hindu festival of Holi and other festivals of the love god, Kamadeva. These games signified the onset of the rains which in India have always been associated with a romantic mood. In ancient and medieval literature, young men and women squirting coloured and scented water at each other brimmed with erotic overtones. The mixing of the coloured water with the right amount of fragrance was a special skill and was done in dedication to Kamadeva.

13—Manicures

Knowledge of nail care was a must for both men and women. Scratching with the nails was one of the most important arts of foreplay (see chapter Scratching in the Art of Lovemaking). Nails had to be shaped and cared for in very specific ways. The nails of the left hand were used for scratching during sex and they were shaped to indicate your capabilities as a lover. As we have seen, for people of high sexual energy, the tip of the nails was filed into points like a saw; for medium sexual energy, it was a point like the beak of a parrot; and for those of dull energy, it was a semicircle like a crescent moon. Ornamented nails were a mark of beauty for both sexes.

14, 15, 16, 17, 18 and 19—Preparing Perfumes, Making Dresses, Garlands, Head Ornaments, Ear Ornaments and Other Jewellery

The arts of perfuming, dressing and the wearing of certain types of jewellery were skills of seduction and had very specific connotations. Every part of the body had to be fragranced with a different perfume because each perfume created its own impact on the senses.

As I mentioned earlier, garlands of different flowers were worn for different purposes and occasions and were a very important part of the shringhar, especially for men. To make love on a monsoon night, you wore a garland of kadamba flowers (it blossoms in the rain and therefore has erotic associations). But a garland of amaranth flowers also signified erotic desire (its petals are tougher and do not shed during embraces and lovemaking).

Each piece of jewellery, too, had its own significance. Certain pieces of jewellery were worn to indicate auspicious days, some were worn for specific sexual positions and some indicated age, availability and marital status. 'Other Jewellery' meant girdles and necklaces. Jingling girdles were worn by women and denoted a very superior sexual expertise. A nine-stringed necklace was worn for the 'sitting' position.

20, 21 and 22—Magic, Charms, Mantras and Conjuring Tricks

Conjuring tricks were one of the suggested games of foreplay and also a prescribed form of entertainment at dinner parties—as a lover or a successful host, you would have to be very good at this.

The last chapter of the *Kama Sutra* is dedicated to magic

and sorcery of all sorts. Any lover worth their salt would have had a very detailed knowledge of lotions and potions to ensnare the beloved, destroy a rival, enhance one's beauty, and so on.

The arrows of Kamadeva are supposed to be strung on mantras or sound vibrations and you could use these mantras to enhance your seduction techniques. After the erogenous zones were stimulated, mantras were chanted to energize the arousal.

23 and 24—Cooking and Preparing Drinks

The way to a man's heart is through his stomach? Not just a man's heart. Cooking and the preparation of special drinks was an essential skill for men and women. It was about being a good host, which made you a desirable person to hang out with—a good party attracted the right kind of people which in turn made you a very desirable lover.

25, 26 and 27—Needlework, Lacemaking and Plaiting Cane Baskets

Being skilled at needlework refers to making garments that made you look bigger or smaller—garments like bras to enhance breast size or corsets to nip the waist. Men wore layered clothes to make their muscles and the groin area look bigger.

Lacemaking was to make designs with crochet or net for ornamentation or bed hangings. Cane was plaited to make seats for lovemaking.

28—Art of Playing the Veena and Drums

Music was essential during foreplay. Bedrooms had a whole

assortment of musical instruments. Of these, the stringed instrument veena was the most important—it produced the right notes for the right mood.

29, 30, 31, 32, 33, 34, 35, 36, 37 and 38—Conundrums, Completing Quotations, Riddles, Developing the Memory, Alternate Reciting of Texts, Puns, Knowledge of the Dictionary, Bookbinding, Storytelling, Quoting the Classics in Answering Questions

Intellect was sexy and brain games were a fashionable pastime at court as well as at parties with friends. Lovers were all the more desirable for their proficiency in these 'brain games'. Incidentally, storytelling was the most important of all these skills. Stories were a very important tool of seduction and an essential part of the foreplay and the after-play. The *Kama Sutra* is very specific on the kind of stories to be told before and after sex. No toolbox of seduction was complete without a large collection of stories.

39 and 40—Woodwork and Metallurgy

These skills were used in making artificial aids for sexual pleasure. The most desirable ones were made of wood or metal. The ability to make them meant you could customize them to your own personal specifications.

41, 42, 43, 44 and 45—Vastu, Knowledge of Stones and Gems, Astrology, Mixing Metals, Interpreting Omens

All these can influence the constellations (grah) and the flow of cosmic energy and through that your vitality, health and your fortunes. For instance, Vastu can guide you on the best way to arrange your room as the season changes in order to increase your sexual energy. Gems, precious stones, minerals and metals are dug out of the womb of the earth or from the deep oceans and so carry the energies of the earth and water. Astrology helps to define your actions according to prevailing and future energies. Reading and understanding omens told you about auspicious and inauspicious days. No lover could afford to be without these skills.

46—Breeding Trees and Plants

Trees and plants were supposed to have magical properties— they could give you everlasting youth, fulfil wishes, help you to remember your previous life, put your lover under your spell etc. They were also used for medicinal and ornamental uses.

47—Quail and Cockfighting

This is probably one of the strangest skills listed in the *Kama Sutra*. Quail and cockfighting were part of the entertainment offered to friends after a convivial gathering. To throw a successful party—the sort of party everyone wanted to attend—marked you out as a cultured man, a man of class and money. This pushed you way up the ladder of desirable lovers.

48—Teaching Mynahs and Parrots to Talk

Aside from being the companions of Kamadeva, parrots and mynahs were considered beautiful and intelligent creatures and were used to carry messages to the beloved or even in times of war. Men of the upper classes bred these birds and it was a part of the gentleman's daily routine to spend at least an hour training mynahs and parrots to talk and sing.

49—Massage

A massage included different types of touching. Massaging the beloved's foot with your own was done in order to stimulate the erotic nerve in the big toe (see chapter Erotic Nerves)—playing footsie, in a manner of speaking. Massaging the head or hair was called hairdressing and included shampooing, plaiting and coifing the hair—very important for ornamentation and seduction. Massaging the body had its own language.

50, 51 and 52—Sign Language, Foreign Languages, Regional Languages

These skills were useful to seduce new partners during your travels.

53—Decorating Chariots

Similar to having a good car—it made you a desirable lover.

54—Fabricating Machines

These were machines used to raise water—an important concern for any householder. A man or a woman who did not understand how to run a good house would not be a good lover.

55 and 56—Poetic Metre, Verses

Poems were written in order to pay compliments in verse with creative use of metaphors and similes. But it was a delicate balancing act—they couldn't be too extravagant and it couldn't be too prosaic, as Bhanu Datta's heroine complains:

> How lucky are those women whose lovers extol
> their mouth or lips, their talk or laugh or grace
> My lover has never seen, heard, thought or dreamed
> Of another woman. What's he to compare me with?[*]

Paying the proper compliment was an art.

57, 58 and 59—Arts of Cheating, Disguise and Gaming

All lovers cheat, all love is a gamble—your proficiency is on how well you do it.

Disguise was an interesting concept in the *Kama Sutra*. To meet the lover you wore dark clothes on a moonless night or white clothes on a full moon night. It was not to hide yourself from other people, but rather from the eyes of Kamadeva, in case he struck you with more arrows and made you even more lovesick.

60 and 61—Games of Chess, Children's Games

To amuse the beloved with different games.

---

[*]*Bouquet of Rasa and River of Rasa* by Bhanudatta Misra, edited and translated by Sheldon Pollock, New York: New York University Press, 2009, p. 65.

62—Good Manners

Bad manners and shrewish behaviour were frowned upon. Refinement in your lovemaking and a deep understanding of the traditions of the time were indispensable.

63—Arthashastra

It was your duty to study and follow this book on commercial success. A poor lover was to no one's taste.

64—Physical Exercise

Physical fitness was paramount. Wheezing, panting or coughing is not what one wants in a lover.

Vatsyayan finishes by saying such were the sixty-four skills that if a woman was left stranded without a husband in a foreign land, she could make a lucrative living out of teaching them. Or if a man lost his fortune he could teach the sixty-four skills to the members of society. Such was the demand for them that not only would he recoup his fortune, but would gain the respect of society as well.

My Advice

The sixty-four skills of the *Kama Sutra* are the equivalent of a modern-day finishing school for men and women. They provided you with the many qualifications which would make you the most desirable companion.

Seduction is not a one-way street. The sixty-four skills were essential for both men and women equally. What was the point of being seduced with exquisite refinement if you couldn't understand the finer nuances of that seduction?

One learnt the sixty-four skills to better one's personality, to become more interesting and accomplished as a person and to increase one's own seductiveness.

Padmashri (in his book *Nagar Sarvaswam*, a tenth-century translation of the *Kama Sutra*) says it is not possible for any individual to master all of these skills and neither should one try and look for a lover who has them, because a relationship with a person like that could only ever end in failure. He tells the story of a man called Ralkumar who happened to have just such a lover; he always felt so inadequate whenever he was with her and she in turn felt so superior to him that in the end the affair between them collapsed in an undignified mess with loss of face on either side.

So the point is not to know everything but to keep working at it—seduction should be a life goal. Particularly as you get older, it becomes more and more important to develop your interests, personality and mind.

The brain is the most erogenous point, intellect is the ultimate turn-on, personality is sexy.

As Padmashri says, a little bit short of perfection is good—otherwise we would become bores.

Acknowledgements

Muses come in all forms.

My mother, grandmother and great grandmother—all highly educated, independent, working women who cemented the road for me so that my journey would be easier.

My utterly special daughter, Tarini—my No.1 fan and supporter. Her pride in my work has made the sun come up every day.

My silently suffering sons (not easy having a mother who works in erotica), Nikhil and Varun, who have applauded me even while dying of embarrassment.

My husband—for suspending his Punjabi-patriarchal-entitled-male identity to keep the home fires burning so I could spread my wings (thank you to my mom-in-law for teaching him well).

My friend and associate, Smita Tharoor, for being my strongest pillar and for cracking the whip constantly—because without her this book would still be on the first chapter.

Bineeta Mitra for forcing me back into the study each time I quit.

Shubham Arora and Minnie Arora for helping translate the

indecipherable Hindi and Sanskrit texts.

Sangeeta Talukdar and Namita Kapoor for flying the flag for me.

The Mysterious S—for being a brand ambassador. You are *the* courtesan extraordinaire.

Monika Mohta, Sangeeta Bahadur, Richa Grover and Sonya Batra for each stepping stone.

Atul Sur for always being a shoulder.

And last but definitely not the least my editor, Simar Puneet, for holding my hand through every meltdown.

Thank you all for making this book possible.